FATES OF THE ANIMALS

PADRIKA TARRANT was born on a wet day in 1974. Her publishing debut came about in *Bunty* magazine in 1982. She read sculpture at Norwich School of Art, where she developed an unhealthy fixation with scissors and the animator Jan Švankmajer. *Fates of the Animals* is her third book, following *Broken Things* (Salt 2007) and *The Knife Drawer* (Salt 2011). She lives in Norwich in a little council flat, with her beautiful daughter and some lovely stuffed animals. She hates the smell of money. She does not entirely trust her cutlery.

Also by Padrika Tarrant

Broken Things (2009)
The Knife Drawer (2011)

FATES OF THE ANIMALS

Stories

Padrika Tarrant

CROMER

PUBLISHED BY SALT

12 Norwich Road, Cromer, Norfolk NR27 0AX United Kingdom

Printed in Great Britain by Clays Ltd, St Ives plc

Typeset in Sabon 10/13

ISBN 978 1 78463 038 6 paperback

1 3 5 7 9 8 6 4 2

Dedicated to my beautiful Jay, and to poor old Dog

CONTENTS

FATES OF THE ANIMALS

Stories

THE MUSIC OF THE FOXES

W HEN ALL THE world was a bald, flat path, the vixen
trotted its length like the grin of a god. Her belly was laden
with the sharpness of foxes; their queer, cruel love and the
waiting souls of all the cubs that she would bear before she
died. So her nails clipped along that empty ground, and for a
century that was the only sound in the whole of the noiseless
earth.

Now the clipping of a fox's claws is a lovely thing, but the
voice of a fox is magic. The song of foxes is harsh and kind
and contradictory; a slipping between beauty and joy and the
jaws that break the marrow from the bones of smaller creatures. The voice of a fox is a shadow in a puddle; dirty and
clean, heartless and full to its surface with love. Theirs is a
subtle beauty; a sly one, like the taste in the air beside a petrol
pump. And when the vixen was bored of the sound of her nails
she stopped and she cried out loud.

The noise that a fox makes when she sings is a *Shak*, shrill
and high; sharp at its core; rich as Ribena. When the vixen
paused, when she lifted her long red throat and spoke, all of
creation held its breath. There was an utter still, and the vixen
licked her lips. *Shak!* sang the vixen, *shak!*

And the air began to stir in a new way, cold and warm
in overlapping billows, full of the tang of winter and the

dwindling sun; perfectly keen. For a hundred years the vixen tiptoed through this new air, bathed in the death and living of the world, the scents and stinks of every creature. It was beautiful. Her slender muzzle split the air before her like the prow of a ship, and the atmosphere that slid along her flank was rank and dark as flowers, tinged with murder and birth-giving.

Then she stopped. The vixen turned to face the way she'd come, the endless nothing of it, like a line scraped in dust with a shoe-tip. And although her nails clipped; although the air was sweet, it was not enough to please her.

Shak! Sang the fox, *shak,* and the night fell down like the opposite of snow. *Shak,* she cried, and the world turned black and streetlight-pale; the moon hung in the sky like a bottle-top and satellites finicked, high above the clouds. The world became a joke of lightness and despair; the creatures chose the dark to bear their young, to hold their stares wide and be afraid.

The vixen lifted her head. *Shak,* said she, and the night glittered with drizzle. *Shak* again, and the nothingness she stood upon became a road; a hard grey road with a lip of a kerb. She pushed her own patterns into it, wrote the network of her nerves in the intricacies of street and alley, of shopping square and churchyard and motorway.

Shak, said the vixen to the tarmac at her paws, and made it echo with sewers and secret rivers and graves. The vixen sang the water pipes and cabling into the matter of the earth, and it was beautiful.

She folded coal into gleaming seams, layers of rock beneath; she sang mud and grass verges, pink tarmac for cycle lanes and grey for the footpaths. *Shak,* said the vixen, and double yellow lines flagged before her and behind.

The vixen sat down then, and her brush curled along her haunch in a long, voluptuous curve. She cocked her magic ears to hear the whispering of bats, the endless chanting of the stars. Then she laid them flat like crumpled cloth and barked. *Shak,* said the vixen, and there were thick square drains of metal; there were manhole covers and litter and rotten leaves.

The world grew rich and cluttered as a dustbin; as the songs in a mind; as the fox cubs in a womb. The vixen sang her hard, sweet song and there was a zebra crossing, thick with paint, studded at the edges, jagged and lovely with zigzag lines. The vixen laughed quietly and trotted across, a steak of rust on white and black.

In the wake of the singing fox were fire hydrants and postboxes and fluttering bus tickets. The cars came after; the nightbus and the glorious headlamps that picked up the red in the vixen's eyes, made them burn for a moment, showed their singingness.

Shak! Spoke the vixen, streaming her song down her back behind the flow of her tail, and everything in the world shone pale and black and red, just as glorious and cruel and full of jealous beauty as can be.

THE HYACINTH GIRL

Y OU GAVE ME hyacinths a year ago. You told me that my eyes were the precise same blue, the mauveishness of veins beneath white skin. And on our very last afternoon the river clung against my bones, cleaved my summer dress against the architecture of me. When my head broke the water, as you lifted it into daylight, the liquid coursed from my mouth and my nose, spread my hair over my eyes.

Water is as grey as the skies, unbreathable; a universe of cloud. The water strokes the skin like a mother's caress, cold as can be.

And although my eyes were hyacinth-blue, although my eyes were still open, I could not see as I had used to. I could not return your stare my love, nor speak your name as the river poured away from me, as kingfishers skewered the water. You braced my chin in the grip of your fingers and you gazed right through me, seeking the soul perhaps, some very last image of yourself in my eyes. And all that I could do was gape back at you, foolish and witless as a poor suffocated fish.

The ankle ensnared by tendril; the tangled stem and petal, the outspread leaves that float like hands, palms uppermost. The burningness of drowning; the cough and cough and cough of it. Months flow by me. The flowers are gone now.

When I became your hyacinth girl I was meat-heavy, loose

4

jointed, feet bare and dragging in the current. When I became your hyacinth girl your very strong hands made welts at my throat, on the back of my neck, each one finger shaped and perfectly blue. My hair knotted round your forearms; I danced against the weight of you, thrashed in the hope of some miracle, some bubble that I might breathe. I lunged and heaved, like a swan forcing skyward with its wings, straining and begging for the air. But I could not be free of you; I could not be free. In time I grew calm.

The summer came and it died despite you and the ribbons in my hair have rotted to grey. There is a nightjar who cries aloud for shame at the coming of the night. In the darkness, still I come to you my love, your hyacinth girl with eyes that never close.

BARKING

THE BARKING OF the dog is relentless as choking, automatic like a door. The barking of the dog fills up the whole apartment, a slow and endless gagging from its pock-marked concrete face and the rubbish-cluttered balcony, from the bone-yellow nets and faded shabby curtains.

This dog has been barking since forever, each note the same, hysteric-shrill, hurting the throat, hoarse and shrieking like a paid mourner. The flat flinches with every note, shudders at the grief of it, of the deadlocked door and the teacup on its side, the contents long bled into the carpet. He lapped it dry ages ago, poor soul, though sugared coffee is no drink for a dog, and now he might lick the droplets off the window, which is turning his breath to water beads, but the dog is stupid and lacks the wits to help himself. So instead he barks, and every cry of his voice hurts like a new-discovered killing.

He trots in little circles, first anticlockwise, then the other way, round and round the armchair, past the television with the sound on mute. He treads his paw against the buttons of the remote control. The channel jumps: it's *God TV*, flogging eternal life. The dog crouches on his haunches and throws out his barking like sobbing.

But *God TV* does not care for the despair of dogs, nor for broken china cups. Neither, these days, does the shape in the

6

armchair, and the dog does not understand. One might mistake that shape for bedding, for a runched-up crocheted bedspread. A slipper lies upside-down against the carpet. The dog lolls his poor dry tongue, and he barks.

THE LITTLE BOY WHO LIED

IN THE ATTIC the air is scarce, and dry as leaves. Trapped between the film and the cardboard, the cracks and the teast-ains and the gelatine-silver years, there is a sepia child in a sailor suit, beads of sweat pricking at his neck. His head is small and slick as shoe polish. He is somehow vacant, unfocussed, as though those eyes were some device of glass and porcelain, like his sister's sleeping-eyed doll that was not lost after all.

They searched a long time for Amelia, lifting bedcovers as gingerly as grave-robbers, Clara, Nurse and him, but Amelia would not be found. They even knelt and prayed to St Anthony, who restores the lost to the faithful. They looked among the things in the toy box and found a poor dead mouse, wedged between the heavy wooden bricks. Clara bore him outside for a proper Christian burial, dangling him from his stiff little tail at arm's length.

He put his hand into the pocket of his short trousers and felt the porcelain fingers that had snapped off like carrots beneath his thumbs. When they ground together it made his teeth hurt. From the window he watched them dig a little hole among the peonies, whose flowers are like fists against the soil. He had tried to break off Amelia's face all of a piece, but she shattered like a saucer. All he had from it was half her pretty smile, twisted in a handkerchief in the lining of his dressing gown.

Her golden hair had ripped right off like a scalp and made his very skin creep; curled and dainty it was, shorn off some desperate woman. He snipped and snipped at it with the sewing scissors till it was just bits, and then he shoved the leavings under the hearth rug.

When Clara came back in with Nurse, he held his head to one side and listened to her weeping. He played with the fire for a minute, thinking of how Amelia's frock, and her tummy, dry as bibles, vanished among the flames with a crackle; Nurse snatched the poker from him and shooed him from the grate.

But the eyes; he squeezed his fingers tight against the palm of his hand. He wanted the eyes. They had sharp edges and were drawing blood inside his hot fist.

There is no birdie to stare in at all these decades; nobody to pity his guilty face, nobody to forgive him, for he is just as helpless as can be, plastered in an album in this attic.

HOW THE DOG LOST HIS WINGS

He was a fine sight back then, white and brown in the paintbox sky, wings and flip-flop ears caught in thermals, flapping like a plastic bag in air. Dog waggled his backside, gleeful as a strangler, and the universe was as full of promise as a bowl of dog meat. He galloped in the emptiness, beating his great furred wings, muscles flexing underneath his pelt, a canine angel.

Beneath his frantic thrashing tail, the earth seemed a small thing indeed, some fanciful toy constructed by the child of a god. Dinky rooftops spread like backbones, edge by edge; the river lay spread-eagled, shining flat beside the trembling sea.

A long bead of drool quivered on the dog's lip, hung in a thread and then plopped off to spatter the world. Below the dog, the petty affairs of men and creatures, cars in car-parks, of rabbits and throwing sticks, were trifles only, barely visible. Beyond his toenails, cats were imaginary specks, thoughts that crawled the ground.

Dog shook his chops, jowls flailing sideways, ears as luscious as spam. There were clouds in his eyes, and dog was meant for higher things than clouds. Dog was a new creation, stirring the sky like exhaust fumes, clever as cyanide, as feathers and candle grease. He meant to have his way with the world, to chew the very sun to fragments.

In those olden days, the planet was a prototype, and the

creatures were yet half-made, waxish at the joints, a little equivocal. Until last week the rabbit had been a proud, leggy thing, till the dog caught him in his jaws and shook him, tore him to rags. It took God a whole afternoon to stitch him back together; ever after he was rather pathetic, hunched low at the ground, legs all set for fleeing.

Lolloping his feet as though he were climbing stairs, dog clambered the sky, through horse tails and Cirrus, to the holy space above them, widdling and whimpering for his very joy. And God was not to be seen, nor angels either, no heaven's host to shoo him away or catch his neck with choke-chain. All around the dog was the undiluted glory of high places; the wondrous light of the sun, weightless as razors.

Dog craned towards it, tried to turn his muzzle to the sun, face to face as though he were its equal. Sunbeams shot through his skull like little knives, dried out the wet at the tip of his nose. Clattering his paws, thrumming his aching wings, the dog found himself transfigured gold. And then, exactly at that moment, the whole enchantment tore right through. Too real, he was, too solid and doggish for that empty rind of air.

And that was more or less the last thing that the dog remembered, as the heat charred away the joints of his wings, as the shining of the heavens turned his eyes plasticky-white. His hairy feathers came unglued from him and his poor wings broke to gristle; the sunbeams all sang their holy songs inside the dog's wretched ears; he dropped like a shot crow, haunch over jawbone over heels. The Dog had moments only to know his fate, to plead with playful gods of flight, as he plummeted between rooftops and peeling flashings; the broken slate tiles and satellite dishes and finally the tarmac; the ravenous tarmac.

THE UPSTART

W HEN GOD WAS asleep, all of creation breathed very quietly; the beasts of the fields and the things that crept upon the earth glanced at each other sideways like sleeting rain, looked down at their feet, the fur and fin and slime of themselves. God knew now that the work of creation was much too hard, and in his dreaming, he fled to some refuge as yet unmade. As he slept, God drooled a little, muttering as all his creation fidgeted, quiet as can be.

Next to God's deckchair were the remnants of a gin and tonic, ice melted and primordial lemon drowned. Drips slid down the glass. There were God's own tailor's scissors, sharp enough for thumbs, sharp enough for the evil hide of crocodile, the rubber skin of hippo.

The sun sank like a pudding as the sky grew red; still God drooled, still he muttered. It was good, as far as it went, but it was such hard work.

Also at God's feet was the wicker hamper that served him as a workbasket; it was trembling from within, as if hatching. Presently the trembling gave way to a kind of rolling till the basket fell onto its side, spilling pins, perilously close to God's own bare and tender feet. He did not stir. Creation stared, wary, all eyes in the coagulating gloom.

The basket lay half open; now it had a purchase against the

side, the thing within pushed the lid until it could sneak out
at last. It turned out to be a monkey's hand, deft and sinewy
and nearly finished. It came out like an uncertain smile, then
turned and groped its way back inside, and the beasts of the
field sighed and shrugged for sheer relief.

But it came back out, this time with a roll of Sellotape and a
large gelatinous eye. Somehow, after a long and painful tussle,
it managed to attach the eye to itself, and suddenly it could see.
It looked and it looked and it looked. And at the low earth, at
the feet of God himself, sat the thing that nobody had created:
snap-wristed with bone and empty arteries, with raw and
brand-new nerves and one squidgy unblinking eye. It sat for a
long time, thinking as best it could.

God stretched out one leg, upturned his gin and muttered
into the collar of his dressing gown, caused all the beasts of
the field and the things that crept upon the earth to hide their
faces for pure fear. God muttered; still he did not open his eyes.

The day was fading fast as the new creature scuttled inside
God's work basket again and tweezered out a squirrels hand,
small and grey as ashes. It scrambled onto the monkey's hand
and climbed up and fell off several times before it achieved
a kind of wobbly balance. The new thing rummaged in the
basket and came out with a needle and a string of gut; it was
the devil of a job, what with the craning of the big hand and
the quivering excitement of the little one, with all the horrified
staring of the proper creatures, each one known to creation,
each one with its own name. If God should see it, this travesty,
this satanic self-created monster, what on his earth would he
do?

Yet in time it was done: two hands, sutured messily, but

sutured nonetheless. It clapped a few times, ecstatic and terrified, then it grabbed the tobacco tins of claws and things; the new creature donned talons.

It so happened there were no legs in God's work basket. The creature discovered most of a fish, however, and imagined itself jack-knifing and slipping through the cold and endless sea. So it gave itself a lovely body, spine and tail and everything, all decorated with tiny silver safety pins and piano wire. But it was a stupid creature, what with having no brain, and try as it might, it could neither swim nor dive, nor even jack-knife. Instead it flapped and flopped on the new-created grass with its new-created thistles and nightshade and nettles that stung.

The creature tired itself out, and lay like some horrible punchline, a spent clockwork toy, with one little surgeon's hand and the subnormal paw of a rodent, pulling at the air.

Then it spotted a set of dentures, grinding themselves; the monkey hand reached out to them, imagining biting, tearing, swallowing. But instead they bit the new thing's thumb and it had to shake and shake and shake to make them let go. The new creature watched, forlorn as the teeth munched themselves a shallow grave in the grass and vanished. The beasts of the field and the things that crept upon the earth, gawped. They turned their eyes to the thing once more, to the ragbasket animal. What if God were to see this? When God loses his temper the very sky might fall.

Meanwhile the new thing was experimenting with wings, and found two that matched for size; one was meant for a chicken, lavishly feathered; the other was a fruit-bat's. The needle kept poking holes in the membrane, till it was just a poor excuse for a thing, like scraps from an umbrella. Even so, it flapped quite well; in a minute or two the thing was an inch from the ground, as its jumbled components strained at their strings and pins and Scotch tape and superglue; all the beasts of the field and those things that crept upon the earth breathed out at once and their breathing rippled the surface of the deep.

The thing had its front end stuck in God's workbasket, gathering parrot feathers. It did not even notice at first that the beasts of the field were closing in on it.

THE HOUSE WARMING

W HEN GOD WAS fed up with creating, he went back to his deckchair and he sat down like a mountain. It was hotter in those days and he was sheened with sweat and knackered. The sun was still high and he hadn't invented hats yet. The air cooled eventually and God crouched for hours, watched the unfolding stars, each pinned in place; here and there were comets, portents of small dooms, and now and again UFO's with nobody to remark upon their stupendous lightshows.

God saw that it was good; nevertheless he needed some place of his own, to store his blueprints and glass eyeballs and swathes of polar bear fur and whatnot. He could have a fridge, and things to put in it. He could conjure a washing machine from thin air and make his holy vestments Daz white.

He got cracking straight away even though it was dark; as there was yet no Ikea, everything, every corner and carpet and toilet and sink plug and electric hob, each was a tiny miracle and God was absolutely shattered. He looked at what he had made this time, and it was lovely. He opened his own front door, trembling with exhaustion, and went up his own gigantic staircase and lay upon his brand new bed. The whole night came and went away again.

Then God's old pal Satan, who knew him from before, trod his way up God's lush garden with the fishpond and the shiny quartz edging. His feet fizzed with every step, for he was much too hot for the poor grass; every foot left the imprint of a small and expensive shoe, made to fit a goat's hoof. The tip of his tail twitched. His Excellency's suit was cut from turquoise asbestos and his little mouth was as vicious as a weasel's. He had a large box in his hands.

Satan turned and looked back down the hill at the land and the sea, at the creatures going about their business like toys made of meat. A goose hung in the air like the ghost of aeroplanes to come, balanced on the brand-new sky, quite perfect upon its feathers. Satan turned to the door again, balancing his box. He managed to push the door bell, which rang like a church and made his Excellency smirk to himself.

God came to the door rubbing his face; he had been woken by the bell; he lugged it open and blinked, finding himself face to face with his old pal Satan. He had forgotten him, his eyes like liquid death and his smile. He stepped up to God like a man selling snake-oil and shook him warmly by the hand, his box balanced carefully against his hip.

Hello, he said, with a voice like an ice-pick, *I heard that you were in the area.* He looked past God, at the Axminster carpet and all the mod cons. *I brought you a gift*, he went on, *to warm your house*, and with a beaming mouth he handed the box to God, who was utterly wrong-footed and took it from him. He muttered his thanks and shut the door in Satan's face.

The box was made of thick cardboard and smelled of burning feathers; the contents were wrapped in blue towelling. He bore it into the living room for a proper look. God peered anxiously as he moved the fabric aside as if he were defusing something. Underneath he discovered a tiny naked boy with

17

eyes like paint and white fluffy wings. He was so beautiful that God himself began to cry. He lifted the creature awkwardly, being unused to babies, and his skin was warm against his cheek, and God discovered that he had been lonely all this time. He unfolded the blue cloth and found that it was actually a garment. The baby reached out, making snuffly noises, and God swaddled him gently.

God wondered what angel children eat; in the end he gave him a bowl of Dream Topping and some pink wafers. He grew into a strapping lad over the course of the evening. This alarmed God a bit; nevertheless he made a little nest of cushions and blankets and settled his gawk-kneed charge upon it. As he tucked him in, the dear little soul called him *Papa,* and he smiled all night, shiny-eyed among the stars in his head.

God awoke late, there being no clocks yet, to the queerest sound downstairs. He crept to the living room, and there was his angel, all grown up, with the cardboard box on his lap. A new angel was sitting inside, giggling as the elder tickled his little round belly. God had never heard laughter in all his life. He perceived that the large angel was wearing the blue cloth as robes; its wings (which by now were neither fluffy nor white) protruded from a slit at the back. The cherub was wrapped in swaddles of his own, arsenic green this time. God stood a long time watching them play, and his eternal heart was warm. Then he went outside to do goddish things, to split the salt and sweet waters; to do something about the crocodile and her marauding infants.

When he came back, there were three; one in blue, one in toxic green and a beautiful newborn swaddled in smoky grey, his chubby face lit up with dozens of very small teeth.

That night they laughed like hyenas and kept God awake. They had found God's liquor cabinet and his fridge soon after. There were five of them by the time God came down for breakfast and they had made an awful mess. A baby was sitting on the carpet with a whole jar of raspberry jam, clutching sticky fistfuls and licking its fingers. A lanky angel with greasy hair was eating the ham slice by slice; he waved at God in the doorway, insolent. *Papa*, he said with something like a smile.

Within days, they over-ran the place, scratching God's records and taking the mickey, trying on God's holy underpants with hoots and barks and screams of laughter. They pretended to be God; they impersonated his voice, his manner of walking. God tried to laugh along with them, to twinkle and chuckle, even to roar and to almost split his sides. Then he went to bed and cried.

God threw the box in the rubbish; they bred and bred from the wheelie bin with their feathers stained with teabags, their raiments soaked in grease. God tried to reason with them, but all they did was point at him and laugh. He tore up the box, but the angels found the sellotape, and still the children came. He buried the box at the foot of garden and they were born of the dirt instead.

He rounded them up, then he miracled huge security gates all the way round his heaven and sent them packing. As an afterthought he set poor dog there to act as sentry.

PIGEONS IN A TIME OF FAMINE

THE WORLD WAS a grey place once, concrete grey and striped with grey. Grey was the sky, and grey the pavements too: clay and stone; clay and stone. The pigeons stretched out their scrawny lives and lived as best they could.

And in that colourless universe, among the puddles and wrappers, they would hop and hunch inside their feathers, waiting for the light to come. Before the dawn, the Anglia Square was a ghetto of pigeons, between the glassy shopfaces, half out of the wind.

Before dawn, there were only pigeons to mourn the city, to pity the bruised sky and the poor mechanical horse, neck arched forever, ready for a useless day of rocking, when a child was placed on its back, when a quid was dropped through its coin slot.

Before the dawn, even its red and blue paint seemed grey; if it could only move for its own self, or stop when exhausted, the pigeons might not have felt so sad. It was a terrible thing to be a pigeon, to spread one's ashen wings and swirl above the shoppers, the black coats and mousy hair; umbrellas fighting with the wind or furled and dripping. It was a tragic life, to scrounge at the corners of the city and feed one's children on pickings and dog ends.

Yet the pigeons were not hateful birds. They wore their

poverty like overcoats; they sat upon the highest places and drizzled the whole world with their compassion. Their souls were dignified as tarnished spoons; pigeons bore witness to the sadness and the tearing of the wind.

Every night they prayed. The god of pigeons was an old woman with a hat thing on her head that seemed to be fashioned from litter and barbed wire. The god of pigeons was kindly like a hot-air vent. She was patient and grey, but bore her greyness calmly for such was the curse of all things living.

The pigeons kept the image of their god beneath the horse, crumpled and ripping from the damp. They rarely pulled her out, in case she was ruined; they knew she was there and that was enough. She was an illustration on some old scrap of linen-paper, crosshatched with creases and dirt. There was curly writing there, and the number 10. That all meant nothing of course, for pigeons did not study letters. They read the writing of paving slabs instead, and the lines of spikes along the Poundstretcher sign. But the picture was their most beloved thing; the god of pigeons warmed their poor grey hearts.

Sunrise lifted the sky as the pigeons prayed, and they softened the morning with their cooing as the light came. And though they did not gaze at her face, the pigeons held the icon of the poor old woman in their great and fluttering souls.

The shops opened all at once and the people came after, to cross and cross the Square, to make the horse nod in arcs as children clung on, almost afraid, as they rocked against its cold mane. It rained for a time, and the rain turned icy, and then for a time it didn't rain; a small girl tripped and hurt herself. The bleed of colour on her shin made the pigeons cry. The Square unfilled with people and the sky turned empty; in an hour more the lights in the shops all stuttered out; alarms were set; doors were locked.

There were only pigeons then, until a couple of kids came to swagger and swear; to hug their ribs and perch on the metal benches. They tried to prise the money from the horse but found they couldn't, so they shared a fag between them and laughed and kicked their shoes, and the look in their eyes was just as grey as can be.

Then one flicked the flint on his lighter, made a little flame leap for one bright moment. The pigeons gasped. His mate pushed at his arm and they shoved each other, bickering, baring their teeth.

Suddenly, there was a crisp packet in the mate's hand, burning and melting away in gouts, and he threw it at the bin with a squawk of delight. It took the boys a while to get the whole bin to catch. The litter was soggy and could hardly be coaxed to burn; in time there was a fire, lazy and gorgeous, licking at the rubbish. Then they looked nervously at one another, and laughed away from the Square with their shoulders slouched, as casually as they dared.

It is a fact that the opposite of pigeons is fire; the opposite of all that ashen life is fire. Fire is all brightness, all rage, a bellow of joy that is gone in a moment. Fire is the blood of the world. The pigeons all shuddered and gaped, and they cooed for glory and fear. And they gathered by the ragged dozen and stared; the pigeons of Anglia Square wondered at this strange pain, this leaping orange pain.

The bin was not very full, and made of metal that would not melt, however hard the pigeons wished; in a little while the flames sank deep inside. The pigeons were possessed by grief at

22

the losing of it; they found themselves flapping to every corner and ledge, picking out tatters of paper, flattened latte cups.

The pigeons gathered small things as though their existence depended on that fire, and with them they fed the flames, begged as only pigeons might that the light and hurting should last a little longer.

So the flames ate up all the stuff to burn in the whole of Anglia Square; there was not very much. All the while the flames grew less and less, and the pigeons gathered closer in.

In all their dusty heads were thoughts of the god of pigeons, folded and thin in her hiding place beneath the red and blue horse. She might burn for a moment, hold the night away for a second or two. But they made no move to prise her out, for pigeons are wise creatures; so they filled the Square with their gentle voices as the night grew cold.

FLYING

I<small>T WAS</small> M<small>ONDAY</small> Assembly and one of my teeth was work-
ing loose inside my face. I was rocking it slowly with my
tongue, although I couldn't bear it. It was horrible, somehow
painful and numb at the same time. Mr Claridge was in his
robes. He smothered his hands over the surface of the lectern,
and leaned into it as he told us our Notices.

Boys, said Mr Claridge, *certain boys, had been seen in the
town centre, still in uniform, brazenly attempting to purchase
cigarettes. These boys, who most certainly knew who they
were, had better be frightened, because they were soon to be
dealt with.* Mr Claridge did his low seethy voice, which was
worse than a shout, because you had to strain yourself to hear
it, and he stabbed his finger against the wooden lectern, so
hard that I had to close my eyes because it seemed certain that
the bone would snap at any moment.

Mr Claridge was tall and narrow and mean as a Stanley-
knife, with blue, translucent eye sockets and a wide thin
mouth. He showed it to us then, his mouth, with a big smile to
indicate that the subject was closed, and then he called us *Boys
and grills,* to prove that he was funny.

I was sitting with my back against the stacked-up edges
of chairs, plastic ones that we mayn't sit on because the floor
suited us better. As my tooth wrenched looser with each move-

ment of my mouth, I felt myself coming loose somehow; rising above my body and looking down. I was very small, and sitting with my fingers underneath the side of my shoe to make them hurt. I always put my hand there, to keep hold of my concentration, so that I could look up at Mr Claridge without feeling him, as if he were nothing but a diagram in a textbook.

Mr Claridge's hair was unwashed and shining with Brylcreem, and a streaky whitish black, like the floor in the girls' toilets. From above his head I could see his padded shoulders and the parallel rakings of the comb. He was talking, and I wasn't listening, and listening was vital in case he told us to stand up or give a show of hands.

Mr Claridge was praying; he lifted his mouth to heaven and pled with God for the innocence of children. He was looking straight at me, and for a while, I was certain I'd been found out. I hung there, in the Morning Assembly air, like a helium balloon in a science lesson: untethered, floating and helpless. The striplights were suspended a foot below the ceiling; they were foul with dust on top, and one held the minute skeleton of a baby bird inside a rag of a nest. Last year, a pigeon had got into the gym hall, and they didn't know because it was Easter. Mrs Parker had come across it when we were getting the trampolines out, all rotten and huddled in the corner, and she'd screamed. Its poor baby, up here all by itself, was tinier and more intricate than a bracelet. My hands were lost below me, but in my heart I cradled it.

Mr Claridge asked that God would make us truly grateful for the luxuries of our lives, and thanked Him that we were not poor starving children like the poor starving children in Ethiopia. He closed his eyes and stretched his arms towards us like a broken umbrella. I was still rising, and found myself forced hard against the ceiling, as though it was bearing down on me, not me on it. God's forgiveness was raining through the roof, dry as a sucked hymn book and hard enough to break your chest. I flailed emptily, tried to heave against the ceiling and flutter down to my self. The flaking paint and cobwebs were all I could disturb; a bit dropped onto Mr Claridge's lectern, but he was busy with our souls and didn't notice.

I suddenly fell when my tooth came out; flooded back into my body with a sickly dribble of blood, and the metal taste of the climbing frame, and the tiny sharp tooth poised between my tongue and the roof of my mouth like a choking seed. My hand was red and hot and hurting underneath my shoe, and then we had to stand up for the Amen; I knew that for the good of my soul I would have to say *Amen* too, even if saying it made me swallow that tooth; even if it made me die. I felt giddy and bottomless as I started to cough, and as fast as I could clamber to my feet, I hit the floorboards again.

DOG'S NIGHTMARE I

T HIS IS THE tale of how the dog was cursed with prophecy. His dream had been a rag-ended one, full of tearing and the thrashing of feathers. He had twisted his back and snarled in his sleep; had kicked and grazed the air with his blunt paws. He had got his own heart thudding like feet on a dustbin lid, steamed his flanks with sweat.

In his dreaming, dog found a white thing, white like a winter sky, all wings and nothing else, flapping in his face as if to spite him, driving him crazy like a skinful of lice. Dog had tried out his patience, but his patience didn't last long.

The air just raved in his face, jabbered and fussed and beat its skinny wings. Dog had thought of useful commands, had tried them out in his head. But the sky would not *sit* or *heel* or *shut its gob,* and dog did not know how to say them anyhow, just play them over to himself as if some invisible master was barking out orders.

Dog growled and barked, and finally he bit at it, filled his mouth with flakes like chickendown. And somehow, quite suddenly, he lost his reason, felt the snapping of some interior leash. He showed the atmosphere his fangs and the drip of his muzzle; he ran in yapping rings, shouting out his fury. In his dream, dog discovered the primal urge of dogs, the blood-hot rage of dogs. Dogs would murder the earth if they could.

So it was that dog caught the whole great sky by the wing; he tore it with his jaws, heaved and tore the atmosphere as it rushed in his ringing ears, dragged it in pieces to the mud of the back garden. It was a massive thing, but in his dream, dog was as vile as a monster. In a minute or less, great gouts of the sky were dropping through the air. Muscular chunks of red and feather fell like dog food, like the spoils of some stupendous crime.

Dog danced amongst them; gore against his chops, against the silk of his coat, his eyes as wild and joyful as a broken windscreen. Still he yapped; still he leaped and he yapped and he tore. When the sky was all killed, when it strewed the garden path and the lawn and the shed roof, only then did the dog shake himself and catch his breath. Then he looked about him with his face all bloody and saw the thing that he had done.

The sky hung off the bones of heaven in rags; beyond them were only the hateful stars and the vacuum between them, only the scorch of solar wind. The planet was naked now, exposed to every prying celestial eye; dog began to tremble. Shame plastered his tail between his legs; dog laid his nose upon his paws, tarred and feathered with the wreckage of the sky, and he whimpered. But the killing was all done, and even a dog understands that things may not be unkilled.

That was when dog woke. He cried himself awake; in the waking instant it was as if he heard some other animal, some poor thing in an infinity of pain. He woke with a rush of pity for this other thing's misery, for dog was not a bad creature, not as some are bad. He did not mean to tear the wings from the sky; his nature had let him down, the wicked awful soul he kept at bay with whining and walking to heel.

When he lifted his head, the sky was not a mess of flesh and veins. The world was all still there, mundane. Dog jumped to his feet and laughed for joy at the back garden, at the muck and the gate and the doghouse. He smiled and sniffed and slobbered his jaws at himself, where some small insect bit him, and pottered round to look in his water bowl; then dog discovered that he understood disaster after all.

The water was rotten and foul; dog tasted the green of his future, the mushroom black of the corpse that waited to become him. He spat and spluttered, and he pawed at the taste, for it was awful. And though the cars still droned out lullabies on the road, though the houses still stood like mountainsides and children played beyond the back fence, dog discovered the end of the world, the stink and clatter and scream of it. He tasted the decay, right there in the back garden; dog understood the fractures that riddled his life, the awful reek of a sky without wings, where nothing holds away the stars.

HUNGRY

Archie's mother died in the most appalling manner; some monster leaving nothing but hair and bits of meat, broken bones and puddling blood. That was how they found him, poor mite, curled inside the dreadful cot of her, howling, nappy wet and heavy. He was smeared in it from top to toe, black and red in his angels' hair. He was packed off to live with his granny, a slight and nervous woman, keen on works of charity.

So the poor wee lad arrived, crying harshly for his mother and for food. In that first night in this strange house, he was barely comforted by cuddles. Granny held him on her lap, feeding him Battenburg cake and Peak Freans until he fell asleep.

His chubby face was gorgeous; it made her think of fat Renaissance babies with wings and fig leaves. His little mouth was a proper Cupid's bow and bright as a lollipop. In his sleep he guzzled at the empty air. He had six rather large teeth in his head, yellow as wood. She cradled him until her legs went numb and the television ended, the test card girl smiling secretly with her clown. And then she had to sit there with him 'til the living room was pitch black, for she couldn't reach the light switch and Archie was quite a weight.

The following night when she sat down with him, she was armed with a fish-slice, so that she should be able to reach the switch when nightfall came. The next day she borrowed a bassinet from the nosy woman from Number 45. She lugged it up the stairs in pieces as Archie scrunched a toffee apple in his monstrous highchair.

By the weekend he was much more cheerful but they had quite run out of food, so Granny had to shove Archie in his pram up and down the aisles at the Co-op. She must have looked a proper sight, anxious and thin in her sparrow-brown coat, balancing a massive basket of tinned ham and apricots in syrup. Archie barely fitted his buggy, squashed in it like a cuckoo. Granny thought he was growing before her eyes, but this must be her imagination. She didn't dare try and catch the bus, not with bags and pram and everything; instead she struggled along Magdalen Street on foot. They got home just in time for tea.

Little Archie was so famished that he grizzled as the shopping was unpacked. He pulled the luncheon meat clean out of Granny's hands and devoured it, never mind bread and butter; never mind even the greaseproof paper. If she hadn't hidden it behind her, he might have scoffed the lamb shank raw.

She dreamed of Archie that night, reaching for her with his sticky baby hands and smiling, licking ravenous lips. She woke with a start to the crashing of the fridge door, torn off its hinges.

AFTER IT RAINED

AFTER THE RAINING, the awful, savage rain, the beast of the field and those that creep upon the earth were devastated. The soft-fleshed armchairs and the barely-hatched motor cars didn't stand a chance; all of these struggled in the flood, floating and bobbing or else sunk without saving. A few managed to crawl from the water; the dog shook his skin and filled the air with droplets. He went scraping and whimpering to God's deckchair, which happened to be on a high patch; God was not there.

It turned out that God was a bit pissed; he had set his gas hob going with a can of beans in a little saucepan and whilst he was there, he turned on the rain tap, a large round wheel that governed the weather. God decided that they needed a refreshing summer storm, to cheer up the things that grow and bloom and make the place lovely. Then, taken by his own virtue as father to everything, he poured himself a little drink and went to his armchair to sip it. In a minute he was asleep.

Silk scarves swam in wonderful shoals, pulsing gently through the water. Pins (hat, sewing and hypodermic) flashed like sticklebacks, spearing what they could. Lanterns and torches and the lights they shine in people's faces to see if they are dead, flashed low at the bottom of the water and blinded the unhappy creatures that live there. Amongst them, the things that dwelt in the black waters, the proper creatures: fish and elvers and seals in their fat fur coats, swam in panicky circles and tried to send telepathic messages to God.

God's kitchen was growing vague with smoke. In time, a whiff of fire came crawling out of the cremating beans, ran its tongue along the greasy worktop, and sidled up to the oven glove. The handle that controlled the rain was still pouring like a bath tap. God woke, coughing like anything, soot in his elderly beard. Smoke coiled around his slippers as the alarm went off screaming like some hideous bird. He threw open the window and caught his breath; realised briefly that it was raining. Several angels sidled up to the door and tried the handle.

It dawned on God that he had better take the baked beans off the hob. He dealt with the fire in his kitchen with a slurry magic spell. A pair of angels appeared at the doorway and God commanded them to clean up. They walked past, sulky; God realised with a jolt that their gowns were soaked right through. He remembered the raining with a gulp and hopped and hurried to the tap to shut it off. He stubbed his holy foot against the table as he went and swore out loud. Through the thinning air he saw the light of the fridge and the grey outlines of the angels as they nicked his beer.

So the rain stopped. The water began to subside by incre-ments. A great deal of time was required to discern the living from the drowned; pairs of spectacles flexed their way along by means of their hinges and did not mind the water at all. Here and there were drifted heaps of digital watches, some with calculators within them and some without, in gasping piles, dying in unison like spent salmon, none of them managing to beep with the hour.

Creatures invented for scurrying, pretty things with fur of pink or orange, perished by and large; the tinies that had not learned about water, and the animals with wings that could only stay flying until they were exhausted, drowned like little golden bumble bees or were snatched by the smart leather gloves that drifted in wait.

God came rushing and limping from the automatic gates of Heaven and stopped, hands over his mouth, astounded by the muddle. The dead of various species lay spent of the banks or floating face-down and window-down on the water's nasty surface. The dying and the desperate called to God for help, for rescue from all this chaos. God, his hands still clutching his face, couldn't bear it; without turning around, he began to back away until he was right up to his front door, and when he reached it he heaved it shut behind him.

INFESTATION

Rebecca found the first: she found it in her bed. Stirring from her sleep, she had turned over, and found scissors against her belly, tucked into the soft fold of flesh that creased when she drew her knees to her chest. Her yelp was loud enough for me to hear it from the kitchen.

She charged down the stairs before I could dry my hands, and she waved them in my face, demanded to know why I had put them there. Rebecca was angry, could hardly speak for crying; I said nothing, just pulled her towards me and cuddled her until she began to still within my arms. After a while we drew apart, and I took them from her, frowning, and went to fetch my glasses from the windowsill.

As scissors go, they were pretty: shiny-bright, and engraved; a tangle of stems and ivy leaves writhed around the handles. The blades were thin and very long; there was lettering down one shaft. The characters were so crazy with curls and embellishments that the actual word was a devil to read.

After an hour of squinting, I decided that it read *LEGION*, although we couldn't guess what this might mean. It took almost as long for me to convince Rebecca that I had not put scissors into her bed. *Why*, I said over and over, *what on earth reason would I have?* My poor girl, in time she brightened up, but I was unnerved. I made us lunch and hung out washing to flap in the turgid air; and whilst she was busy with her drawing I turned out the cupboards to keep myself busy. The afternoon went on forever, the light was pale and greasy; the sky drained at nine, and night appeared, resentful. The light bulb was dull as the dusk; in the end we put the TV on just to cheer up the living room. Matthew Kelly filled the silence with colour and tinned applause.

Eventually, I made myself a drink, and went to draw the curtains; the window was shut, but still the heady stink of too many flowers in the garden made me giddy. The lane was still half-lit, and birds were singing.

I pulled the drapes shut and returned to my seat. There, in my mug of tea, was another pair of scissors. It was as if they'd sucked the life out of it: the liquid was suddenly tepid, but the scissors were too hot to hold. I tried to pick them up, but dropped them as I felt my fingers burn. They fell back into the cup and knocked it over. Rebecca tucked her feet underneath her on the settee and shuddered.

It was too hot to sleep that night; it was always too hot, and the rot and the sweetness everywhere made the bed damp and my head throb. I read Rebecca a story, though she was too old for stories, and I tucked her into bed; I made the poor little soul wear three thick blankets, and bedsocks as well, as though the layers might protect her from sharp things, unless she died of heat first. I heard her for hours, sighing and coughing, but eventually she was quiet.

I lay in my room, a hypocrite with no bedding, listening. I must have dozed eventually, for suddenly I woke, aware of a noise: a chittering like dozens of nickel crickets, little scissor blades scissoring in unison. A flash of metal by the door made me leap to my feet, my bare, soft feet. I ran to Rebecca's room.

As I rushed in, there was a sudden, shocked hush, as if I had interrupted some complicated ritual. There she lay, her head on one side, surrounded by scissors; hundreds and hundreds of scissors. Her hair had been cropped from her head by the handful; thick chestnut locks lay on her pillow and the floor. They'd begun to nibble at her bedding too: frayed snippy holes had been dug into the bedspread, each one pierced by the nose of a blade. Rebecca groaned, and only half woke up when I heaved the blankets aside and hurried down the stairs, staggering under her weight.

I took her into the living room, plonked her onto the sofa, and fled to the scullery where we kept old shoes and cleaning stuff. I turned my Wellingtons upside-down, (shaking out five silvery monsters), and I put my feet into them. I felt a bit safer, and I grabbed my yardbrush and went back to my daughter.

She was curled up like an embryo, rubbing her eyes and whimpering. I leaned over and kissed her forehead, and I pulled out all the furniture and searched the room until I had swept every last damn pair of scissors out into the hall. I shut the door, and together we got as comfortable on the settee as we could. Despite myself, I fell asleep.

I wonder what I should have done for the best. I tried so hard to keep us safe. By the time the dawn came, the grating of scissors was loud enough to hurt our ears. The door began to creak at the pressure against it from the hallway. Rebecca did not cry, nor complain, but put her hand in mine and led me to the window.

The garden was as lush as cancer, and the clematis crossed

and crossed over the window-frames in fragrant knots of wood, like the bars of a fairy tale prison. As we stood and watched, it grew. I held my daughter close against me, and we looked towards the garden and not at the splintering, slowly collapsing door.

LOST

SOMEHOW, I MISLAID my mother: left her somewhere, or let her escape like a heartless little bird. I looked to see if she had crept into the space beneath my bed, and there I met a tiny monster who was scared of me. He let me see the nest that he had made, all out of dust-fleece and the lyrics from pop songs. He hadn't seen my mother, though he showed me a Silver Jubilee coin.

I looked for my mother in the smoking room, to see if she had slipped behind the cushions, flat as a letter. I saw Madeleine in her special chair, rolling a tinful of fags and tuning the radio. There were messages between the stations, but none were about my mother. She wasn't in the ashtrays, and Madeleine hadn't seen her.

I snuck past the nurses' station quietly; glancing at the desk in case they'd put my mother in the Pending tray. She wasn't lined up with the pencils or the empty coffee cups; the thumb tacks were telling each other sharp little lies. I listened as long as I dared, which wasn't long enough.

When I sniffed the air, my mother wasn't in it, not even a molecule of her. I tried to remember what she looked like, how she had been. All I could call to mind were glasses and hair, and the sound of the kettle boiling. She wasn't squashed on the carpet like a biscuit crumb, and I was sure I couldn't taste her.

I went to rest my elbows on the windowsill, jostling for space among the dead flies from last year, and I saw the hare-brained afternoon chasing around in circles in the grounds, and then I had an idea. I ran as fast as fast, back to my bed space, the soles of my feet slapping the floor tiles.

Now I was sure that I was in luck. I stripped off the blankets on my bed with a triumphant gasp, but instead I found myself there, with my eyes half open and my teeth showing, tainting the atmosphere with an aftertaste of sleeping pills and malted milk.

MEAT

T HEY ARE WAITING. They are meat. Tenderly coaxed by knives, slit from throat to belly, hung by their hooves; despair in their drippings, flaps and folds of skin.

Gently, lovingly, they are divided from one to many, hock and knuckle; flank and haunch; useless twirly tail and murderous head. So it is that there are many of them, the bits and cuts that used to be a single animal, every one suddenly a separate thinking thing. They were never so clever as they are now.

There is a part that is desperate to escape, to have it away on its sharp little feet, to feel the concrete and the blood beneath its trotters. It is not possible to run when one is suspended, turning amongst the viral motes of August.

The ears can hear the summertime going on without them, ambulances and the wailing of seagulls beyond the meshed windows. They're out of their minds now the brain's cut loose, every portion of them bloodless since they were emptied into a bucket. Their viscera came away of a lump, and with every lump and chunk they became yet more divided. They have been sliced into this and that, the prime and the cheap joints, ghastly pink sausages and twists of hide for dogs to chew.

There is a part that is ravenous, belly as empty as staring, without one single thing inside. There are neither guts, nor heart, not liver; nothing. It wishes to devour the world, and quickly, please quickly, because it is so hungry.

There is a part that wants to kill, to open its bloody maw, screw its eyes and sink its fangs into the men in spattered Wellingtons, into their strong and red-flecked arms. But champing against empty air is torture for the jaws.

Poor things, they hold their peace, for if they were to cry out, that stuck pig scream, if they were to yammer for wholeness, then they might shriek the whole place down; reduce this dying to the very essence, the tiny nightmare at the heart of the slaughterhouse. They might just scream the butcher and his mate into ghastly sausages and cheap and choice cuts, every one of them lovingly divided between skin and dog-bones, slit from throat to belly. They are very sad.

SMILE

THE CHESHIRE CAT'S all made of face, happy as a mouth. The Cheshire cat is teeth and wires and jester's eyes and patchy orange fur. He stalks the unlit neighbourhood when the world's all passed out drunk, and only the pigeons are awake to coo in terror. Then he parades between them with his grin and his tail in the air, dislocated at the tip and all askew.

The Cheshire cat quite owns the place and knows this very well; at night he comes for the souls of sleepers, crawling through the chinks in windows or posting his smile through the letterbox and his body after.

When the Cheshire cat stalks up flights of stairs, his paws are hard and very small; on unvarnished wood they tap-tap like a white stick. Against carpet they make no sound at all, but the shadow on the landing wall is raggish and awful.

And you, in your bed, hear him. The ears of sleeping folk are full of nerves; can hear a thing to be afraid of through a thick wall, through the opposite end of the town. But your body does not twitch a finger, for your soul is not in it.

At night the souls of sleepers creep from them; they nibble in the silence and worry at the peeling paint on the skirting boards. They tremble and skitter and they climb the bookcase, hunting for the picture in that album that you don't remember, the colour-plate or line of poetry that makes your life make sense. They fret and scritch for the photo between pages, for the paper-fragile marigold picked from the garden by ancient children.

So you sleep with your body curled small as your true self fiddles at a magazine that's stuck behind the books, where the hardbacks are jammed perfectly tight. Its tiny ribs are hammering now, for the tipsy stink of the Cheshire cat is slouching down the landing. Your soul pauses like porcelain as you breathe, as you leak sweat against your pillow.

When he comes, he comes piece by piece, a row of little triangles and two wet eyes. And when his face is ready, after a slither of skin, and paws spread flat like blue-prints; his broken tail comes last of all. Then he is there, the cat and the grin together, nicely assembled, scarcely even a join. And he jumps.

But your soul is quicker, quick by just a thread, so it streaks its way right up the bedspread, barely in time. And before the Cheshire cat throws his rag-ends forward, it is off in a little blur of white, into your open mouth, inside the secret nest where your spirit hides from cats. Your heart leaps in the night time and your eyes flick wide.

INSTRUCTIONS (FOR A GAME)

1. Clear a space on the carpet, with room enough to admit the seated players and the game. Ignore the birdsong outside and the mindless grinding cars. Close all doors and lock the windows. The net curtains will suffice. Open the box and lay out the contents; check that nothing is missing. The box has been trodden on; repair the corners with winding Sellotape. Count out the false money and the toxic lead-cast counters; the Chance cards are like tarot: greasy, dangerous. The board is tattooed pigskin; the die is small and terribly sharp. The youngest player takes the first turn; play continues widdershins.

2. The game begins with the first seven of the die, the thrower ascending the ladder to the appropriate square. There at the top of the snake that will take him down a peg or two. So he climbs and finds himself slithering backwards straight after, down the butter-slathered serpent that lurks there, the fall that lies in wait for the pride.

3. One must become a plastic mouse. Lots are drawn according to the fracture of wishbones in several rounds, until two players remain. The little one must act as referee. The bone must be held onto by the smallest finger of the left

hand. The longest fragment remaining indicates the player that must turn into a mouse; the metamorphosis must be completed within ⅘ of a minute or else the player is disqualified. The mouse may be pink or blue according to gender of the chosen participant. The mouse may not continue in the game, but must be given a nest of sorts; money from the Bank may be shredded into a margarine tub and the mouse shoved into it.

4. One must become the son of God, unless he holds an exemption card. He must wear a paper crown and endure the spiky glancing of his disciples. He will hear chickens and nobody will ever look him in the eye, staring instead at the bleeding heart of him like some cheap table lamp.

5. One grows old and the others devour him, every scrap, lungs and wig and everything. Old age has settled in his lap like the opposite of a cat: cold and loveless, purring like despair itself. In seconds he is hardly more than a hearing aid and the players will lick up his very dust. Their faces will smear with perspiration and a greyness that will never wash away.

6. The Thing that makes the sun come up is very small, and ghastly-black, because it absorbs the gigantic night so that the day shows up. The players must throw the Thing to one another, proceeding clockwise to the tune of *London bridge is falling down, falling down, falling down*. When the music stops the player left holding the Thing is enveloped by darkness and is never seen again.

PADRIKA TARRANT

7. The smallest player must cover his eyes and count to one million as the rainwater spreads down the window, as the universe spreads an inch thick upon the carpet. The game concludes when the Bank is empty; when the world is all used up; when God himself squats on his immortal knees and sobs. The players divide the remains between themselves: nothing and nothing, multiplied and divided by nothing.

ANGELS

I SEE ANGELS EVERYWHERE. I can't bear it. The children's Bible they used to give out at school for RE had the whole thing wrong. The pictures aren't bad, they're right about the golden hair and the wings and raiments and everything, but the faces in the colour plates are always friendly, and pious, and godly, and all that. They never show an angel sniggering. The thing about angels, the main thing is that they are filthy. Their wings are long and graceful, but they're mottled greys and browns, and all patterned like pigeons' wings. You do see the odd white angel, but they're just the half-blind albinos the bigger ones torment.

Angels give off an unearthly light, it's true; like a street lamp. They wear long pale gowns until they're ragged with tears and fag-burns and foul as floorcloths. No wonder they're spiteful.

I heard once in the playground that if you sit at your dressing table on the stroke of midnight and light a candle, the devil himself will stand behind you and look into the mirror. It was Lauren who told me; she said her sister had tried it. She only said so to see what I'd say. I told her it wasn't the devil really, it's angels, but she laughed, and told her friends I was mad, and the bell went for registration.

Actually, she was half-right, because the devil is only

another one of the angels. He's a fallen angel, the chaplain says, but I don't know what that's supposed to mean. Maybe he's on drugs: heroin; not medication. I don't really see how you can get much lower than common angel, to be honest.

People don't see angels very often, because once you start there's no getting rid of them. They get in your face, after you've seen the first one. They stare at you in the plastic windows of the bus shelter or the shine off the newsagent's spectacles when she gives you your change. They stare, and they smile, and they drive you nuts.

Angels are like crows; they descend on anything shiny. They look at me from shop fronts and bits of broken glass and television screens and goldfish bowls and spoon backs and they laugh. They're in the behinds of things: the spaces between walls or puddles on wet days. They crowd behind the sliver on the mirror and they laugh.

When I used to live at home, I had a dresser, pink it was, all covered in thick gloss, with one hair from the brush trapped and drowned in the paint like a wasp in treacle. I put my Barbie stickers on the drawer fronts, and the Well Done sticky I got for a story that I wrote about my dad. I only ever got the one Well Done sticky. I did try though.

It had three mirrors on it, the dressing table, a big one at the front and two other little ones with screechy hinges. When I was nine, I put my head right inside; my face was up against the big mirror and I scraped the sides in until they were touching my ears. There were ten million eyes, and so many faces, that I completely panicked and all the angels screamed. Somehow I kept holding the sides against my head, and I tried to free myself but I couldn't and all the angels howled at once.

I cried so hard that it's like when you can't get enough air and your breath comes in great huge sobs. My mum asked me, *whatever is the matter?* And I couldn't talk properly to reply, so she just said I was silly, and then something important happened on telly so she told me to *shush*. My mum said I was being stupid, but I wasn't being stupid at all, it was the angels. That was how it started.

It isn't easy to keep on top of everything; if you can't see past the grinning angels to check your hair in the mirror, you look a bit of a state. That kind of thing tends to make you stick out and then you're given a hard time. I did my best; still do, but even so, it's tricky. When you add all the noise on top of that it's awful. They chatter and giggle all the time, and they point at you and whisper.

When I tried to sleep in my old room at home, all those bloody wings made a thrashing in the air, and they'd recite the Lord's Prayer in their sarky angel voices. If they saw they'd got to you, it would get worse. Obviously, I kept the mirror covered, but if you think about it there's so much shiny stuff in the world: the windows and belt buckles and patent leather shoes and the dog's eyes; you're never, never alone. Because they glow, I have to sleep with a blindfold on; and they're dirty, so they stink of vomit and lighter fluid. I never have got used to it.

There was one day, the last day I ever went to school, when it dawned on me. Well, if you're having to cope with angels all the time, the last thing you need is a circle of people calling you names. It was Lauren who started it; for the whole of the morning break she kept on about my greasy hair; called me a loony over and over. It was raining, and the asphalt was soaking and glittery, with angels in every single drop. Well the angels just loved it, didn't they, and they joined in, staring out from the rainwater and wetting themselves laughing. It got so loud that I had to make the angels stop before I went mad, so I turned around and jumped on Lauren.

She hit the playground like a wet sack, and she began to scream, and then the noise was even worse, so I picked up her head by the hair and smacked it against the tarmac. Someone started throwing up; a girl went running for a teacher, but the angels had stopped laughing; they just looked at me, shocked and silent. I felt quite weird and dreamy as I walked away.

There was a sound like beating wings in my ears as I drifted through the gate, and by the time I got into the city I had to concentrate hard to keep my feet touching the ground with each step. In the end I was exhausted with trying to walk, so I sat on a bench in front of the old KFC. They were doing it up; the fitters had washed the windows all over with white stuff on the inside.

When I looked there was an angel there, just the one, sitting with her feet apart and her knees together. She looked ever so sad. I thought she must have been hurt; she was cradling one hand against her chest and her hair was all plastered over her face. She was hardly glowing at all. Her wings were mucky brown and only half folded; the one on the right looked broken. Angels can't really fly you know, only flutter: they're a joke of nature, hybrid things that struggle to tread the earth, but can't get airborne either. No wonder they're spiteful. The thought of it makes me cry.

DOG FINDS OUT WHERE
KNIVES COME FROM

T HE DOG WAS keen to bury his bones before God discovered the rabbit was missing again. He filled his hairy feet
with earth, felt the mud between his pads. For a time it was
all rather jolly, with the sky overhead like a smotherer's pillow,
the black of peat against the AstroTurf green.

Then his joyful, raking paws came to a halt against a thing;
a long object that was not a bone; that was not a rock or anything that lives beneath. He snuffled his nose at it, sneezed his
way along its length, half of which was wood, which is the
meat of trees. Dog nibbled at it, just to be sure, and discovered
the blade. He was dumbfounded at this, for stainless steel is
not the meat of wood or mud, but a thing that grows in evil
places, deep in the swollen earth, a slender demon that slit the
poor dog's mouth and made him bleed, even though it did not
have any teeth.

COLLISION

O N THE PARANOID boundary between market and hay market, Starbucks smiles bright as dentures. You have been standing here for ages in a queue that's barely moving; you gaze at the man in front. He is wearing something with a hood; there's a logo on the back like feathers. He turns and you see him in profile and you discover that he is not a man but a beautiful boy, thin-chested and blond. He looks right through you. Somehow the sight of him makes you ill.

He wants an Americano. No milk. Grande. For drinking here. You shuffle into his vacated spot; you have memorised your order and you trot it out like a child in a spelling test, and a moment later you pay. You make your careful way up the stairs and gaze around the room. There is one place free: a massive leather armchair with a window view. It is opposite the Americano boy. You balance your way over and sink into the seat, put your tray between you both. You have a smile prepared, and you glance up, ready to be a little apologetic, but he is staring out of the window, wide-eyed, grinding his teeth. For a second or two he looks quite unearthly, despite his coffee and his hoodie. You take him in in glances: he is all dressed in grey, without a coat, although it's raining. His eyes reflect the window and the pigeon spikes.

Lunchtime slides past as if on wheels. You are still nursing your latte, though it's cold now: the boy has not touched his drink at all. He is staring, right outside at the air and the rain; his lips begin to move and you decide that he is only mad after all. Still you watch him in gulps, the way one coughs down medicine.

You reach for your tepid coffee at exactly the moment that the sea gull strikes the window; smashes the glass; smearing blood against it; making a perfect bull-eye of cracks, the fat snapping of quills and bone and guts and stuff, the wretched thing magically turned from daylight-white to horrible red. It's the skull that burns you most of all, staring at the boy and you, broken beak agape as if it had swallowed a fish hook and been dragged here. Then all the lumpy mess slathers down and off toward the ground, leaving the awful broken window and the print of a bird, wings akimbo like an angel's.

You are terrified for a moment, as the boy stops his muttering and turns to smile at you. You grope to your feet, coat and handbag and everything, as he drains his coffee and begins to chant again.

DOG'S NIGHTMARE II

A MOMENT LATER AND dog is transfigured, spread against the sky like so much tracing paper. Now he's as flat as can be, all dryness and hurting and threadbare curly pelt. Dog is the air at nightfall, corner to corner, scrabbling for a purchase on the horizons, wet with the seas that pour off the world. Dog coughs up the moon like a hairball, chokes the heartless sun back down his throat, even though it's hot as anything.

These days dog's famished as a drum-skin and the constellations are woven into the underside of him and his empty trembling belly. His spittle makes the rain; the dreadful hunger in him brings about the thunder; when he weeps whole cities drown.

Sometimes the angels come to visit him; to flick his massive nose or call him nasty names or to yank his poor defenceless whiskers.

THE GUILTY

THE WHOLE WALL is Plexiglas and it reflects only slightly, vague so the killer can see the tarmac and the shuddering neon light. The car park is hooded with the night, as though it cannot bear the sight of him.

The killer dips his face to his cup, trying to swallow boiling tea. He sees the shake in his hand as it quakes the liquid like the surface of primeval waters. He lifts his cup as though he had never seen such a thing before: the soft give of the polystyrene and its pitiless whiteness. He has a hangnail; he puts his cup down with a slop and he digs his teeth at it, catches the edge in his mouth and rips it away. A small bubble of blood gathers at the quick and it gives him the horrors; he rubs his fingers against his other hand, smearing it to nothing.

When he looks up there is a rook, standing by itself on the other side of the window, gazing, staring at him as though he could see the killer's aching skull. The rook turns sideways and blinks, and its blinking makes the killer shudder and catch his lip between his teeth.

She might not be dead. He hadn't set out to hurt anyone. But he had to stop her screaming, that awful shrieking that was almost a roar. The noise is ringing in his ears like a rubbish pop song, like a slipping fan belt. He presses his eye sockets with the heels of his hands; sees flashing lights for a second.

The rook is still sizing him up, squatting on his thick stiff legs, greyish beak pointing at the killer as if one jab might undo him to scraps like rotten knitting.

Perhaps she is fine. Perhaps she has woken up by now, having surged from the bathtub, just in time to take a massive breath. Perhaps she has found his towel. Perhaps she has just gone home. He hadn't meant to hurt her, he tells himself. But oh (the thought of it makes him catch himself in his arms), what if she has told on him? What if the police were to find her hysterical and dripping in his front hall? What if she were discovered, still as a sleeper, her hair billowing round her face? He would have to explain; it was all a dreadful misunderstanding.

The rook hops toward the plastic window, towards the shoe of the killer, which is drenched like his T-shirt beneath his jacket. It turns his glossy back as if sickened. The killer stares at this bird, this jumped-up judge and jury both, and for a long time he feels as though he should make excuses, should just get this vile black bird to comprehend what had happened, how none of it had been his fault, not really.

It turns back to the killer now, whose body begins to needle sweat in little points upon his face, his armpits. The rook knows perfectly well what he did; rooks are magic, and can see the future.

RATS

THEY STEAL YOUR thoughts, these rats with muzzles like forks; they steal everything that you are. I risked a careless smile last week; let it slip when I pulled the curtains back and saw the snow. A rat with nothing in her eyes sliced it clean off my face and snuck behind the sofa with it. I found its bones there, two days later, scavenged and scraped to an empty curve.

I'm almost sure that I had a dream this afternoon, perhaps of love or flying; when I looked for it later it was gone, and all there was were the scrunching of tiny white teeth through bones.

There are rats in my house, in the spaces inside the walls: more than the maggots in a bait-box, small as talking and impossible to kill. They stain the wallpaper, and if I take my eyes off them for a second, they'll snap my mind into slivers and they'll bury me beneath the carpet's underlay.

I used to have a name, you know; I have had loads of names, but the moment I stop looking at the rats, they rob everything away again, and leave me with their shrill laughter and the swipe of their naked, scaly tails.

DE LA VIANDE

Entreés: Pâte de fois gras: Moules à la Français

Plat: Jambe d'un Homme Sophistique et Riche, avec Chaussure Marine; Légumes Verts, Carottes Jaunes et Petits Pois.

Déserts: Sorbets ou Fromages

The establishment is rather select. Generally speaking, the waiting list exceeds six months in advance; and of course, tables are only allocated on the basis of invitation from the management. Still, in view of our little party, certain strings were pulled, and an exception had been made at the discretion of Chef himself.

Discretion is the watchword, one might say, of La Palais. Indeed, our little *bijou* is so very select that society conducts its small affairs right outside the premises, without so much as a suspicion that La Palais exists. We are, one might say, under their very noses while they stuff themselves with burgers and various filth.

The operation itself had been conducted some four weeks previously. I am told that the time delay is vital, as this rarest of dishes must be left to rest, to hang, to mature. To rush such a gastronomical endeavour would have been nothing less than

blasphemous. The service provided had been simply laudable;
I was attended to by diligent and respectful staff. My sur-
roundings had been more than comfortable; I was in and out
in a week.

We arrived a little before eight, and already many of the
tables were occupied. A genteel swell of conversation had gathered in the air, balanced by a pianist who filled the room with
a soothing undercurrent of jazz. As is customary for all non-
members and for those not bestowed with a permanent con-
tract, he was wearing a blindfold. It was generally remarked
upon that this rather showed off the prodigious quality of his
musical skill. I was hailed warmly by all: these are my friends,
those of a truly like mind.

Francois was at our side in a moment, collecting coats,
umbrella and crutches, and spiriting them away to the cloakroom. (I have it on good authority that the garments are in fact
placed upon mannequins; certainly, I have never had anything
returned to me with the slightest wrinkle.)

Nicola was charming, dressed exquisitely and eager to listen
to my stories. My anecdotes, I must own, are rather renowned;
yet as I always say, it is at least in part the quality of the audi-
ence that maketh the speaker. Dear Nicola, she brings out the
best in me. She embodies the absolute quality of La Palais; one
might almost forget that she was employed here, but for the
dainty silver padlocks. And then it was a quarter past eight
precisely. Dinner time. I was fairly fluttering with nerves.

The main course was, naturally the principle attraction.
The tureen was borne in by the maitre d' himself. It is the
house custom to carve at the table. His reverent entrance made
quite a spectacle; it was placed between the two of us with

a flourish,, and the whole room fell silent in anticipation. I must admit that I revelled a little in the attention. Nicola was slightly flushed, lips parted, radiant.

There was a tiny intake of collective breath as the lid was lifted. Chef had outdone himself. It was quite wonderful, and with the most understated of presentations, a swirl of red and green coulis just glazing the plate. The joint had been finished with a paper rosette of pristine white; as garnish, the shoe, crocodile leather and marinated in lavender honey, was in situ rather like the magnificent wings of a roasted swan.

The entire house burst into applause; I bowed my head, embarrassed, pleased merely that my turn had come to make my own modest offering to the Club at La Palais. The founder, a venerable octogenarian and gourmand of world renown, called 'Bravo' to me from his wheelchair. Although obviously he was unable to clap, Maria, his Nicola, you might say, was on hand to fulfil this function on his behalf, and when the time came, would assist him with his meal. Oh, such an evening! The maître d' unlaced the shoe with a deft flick of the carving knife and began to razor off the first mouth-watering, fragrant slices, a feast for all. A triumph. Dear me, yes.

THE DISAPPEARING

From the day of my Victoria's birth, I felt that somehow she was not to be mine for long. When I was delivered of her, I slept for hours, and towards the morning, finally waking, I glanced up at the dripping window and saw an owl gazing in at me, calm as death, the sill scarred by his great shearing talons. He shrugged his wings and beat slowly away, leaving me to stare at the forks of water streaking the glass. I turned my face to the child in my arms and wept.

My house learned the voice of my baby, leaned itself like an old dog against the sounds of her laughter, and grew warm. Time turned the colour of her eyes from infant-blue to the copper-brown of pennies. Her hair, when it came, was red.

Victoria grew, as children will, but at two years was a tiny creature, and oddly poised upon her feet, as though to walk was a strange imposition upon her body. Still, she ran about the house and would play with an almost feral abandon; she sometimes seemed as closed to me as that of a sleepwalker, but then she would light up like summer and tumble into my arms.

There came a day, when Victoria was almost three, that I could not find her. I searched for her, rushing from room to room in sudden panic, until at last I yanked on the back door, and stepped out so fiercely that I all but fell over her. The air was glutted with clattering wings and I held my palms over my ears and screamed as a thousand little birds burst the air about me. There, in the puddling shadow as they all dashed skywards, sat my girl, a long magpie's feather grasped in each chubby fist, waving them both in the air and chuckling with a baby's glee. As the Virgin had done before me, I took this thing and held it to my heart.

I do confess that from that time I clutched my child to me like a miser, wrapping each moment in muslin as though I thought I could hoard time in waterglass or dry it on a sunny window ledge like the head of a teasel flower. Victoria matured a little with each day, but remained a slight child, prone to silence, tousle-headed. I kept the doors locked; at night I heard birdsong, dripping and beautiful as mercury. My daughter slipped through my life like a ghost, like the half-seen reflection of some other child.

And then, she began, quite of a sudden, to hum, an ethereal, glassy song without words that dropped through my consciousness like a hot spoon in lard. I was so entranced that it was not until days had gone by that I realised she had stopped speaking altogether. I clattered pots in the kitchen and bellowed out hymns from Chapel in my rough old voice, as if I might make enough noise for us both.

Often I would follow the singing into this room or another, and see Victoria gazing out of the window, her shoulders shaking fit to break. I would march forward myself, and see the glass grow black with flapping as the little birds took flight. Victoria would shrug and walk, swaying, from the room.

Then there came a time when the birds did not leap into the air at my approach any more. I stood beside my daughter as she stared like a martyr into a pitiless wall of syrup eyes, heads

63

cocked sideways, clever as fire. I waved my arms and shouted at the window. Victoria flinched sideways and the birds did the same, billowing like a breeze through a wheat-field. Nerves recovered, they stilled and resumed their secret vigil. I snatched the curtains shut.

That night I drowned in nightmares, clawed at the bars of a bell-shaped cage, until the million tiny fractures of the dawn chorus began to split the darkness. With a start I woke.

Sick with premonition, I crept to the window and looked without surprise at Victoria, translucent as doves in her night-gown, walking with palms stretched towards the swollen morning.

I came downstairs slowly; I did not run to the back door, nor was I surprised to see that the lock had been pecked out of the wood by hundreds of little pecking beaks.

The dew-sodden grass bore the print of her bare feet: one step, two and three, and then no more.

MAGPIE FALLS IN LOVE

T HERE WAS ONCE a magpie who would sell his very soul
for a bit of cheap tat. He lived in the high gutter of a derelict
nightclub, and he kept his petty hoard wrapped in a silk hanky
that he stole from a poor old clergyman.

Now, the magpie adored his treasures; thieving was the only
thing that made him happy; that and preening his wonderful
plumage. The magpie spread his wings like glossy fingers, and
admired his white and black good looks; he remarked to the
empty air of his lucky fortune: to be both handsome and wealthy.

The magpie arranged his cloth on the moss-rotten downpipe, and with his cunning beak he laid out his wealth. These
included: the top from an ancient pint of Jersey milk; a little
lead boot from a Monopoly set; a broken silver crucifix, and a
bodkin, as blunt and bright as anything. The magpie winked
his eyes and grinned amongst the traffic stink.

Well, it happened then that a teenage girl walked by, below
him and across the street, and stopped, staring into the road
where they were digging it up. She was a beautiful thing, with
hair of raven deep and cheeks as white as scouring powder,
and she was bunking off the last two hours of school. She was
easily as lovely as a string of beads, maybe even as a DayGlo
effigy of Christ himself. The magpie gazed upon her pretty
face, and fell catastrophically in love.

The black and white child stopped at the kerb, and craned her head around the roadworks, trying to see if the way was clear to cross, but a rumbling yellow generator blocked her vision so she tutted and pressed the button on the crossing three times. The magpie was transfixed, and knew that his heart would be hers forever. He tried to catch her eye from his grandstand perch; he struck a pose for her, giving her his best side, his most worldly, knowing look. She peered at her watch, tried to see the road, and pushed the grubby button one last time. She paid the magpie no attention; did not even glance up at him.

The magpie was horrified. How could such a beauty not seek its like; how could this ethereal creature look about and not spot such a splendid bird? She cared nothing for the magpie and his adoration. He felt himself humbled; drawn up short. How could he have been so vain? He hung his head for a moment, little brain ticking, then brightened up. A gift! He would woo his idol with a gift; she would share in his wealth and sit with the magpie atop the moss rotten downpipe. And none was better placed to give than he, the wealthy prince of Cattlemarket Street.

So the magpie turned to his shining stash, and lifted up the golden milktop with reverence. He cast it down to his love, but a breeze caught it and rolled it off sideways; it hit the road behind her without even a noise. The magpie cried out loud for his despair. But any prince can give mere riches; perfect adoration is nothing short of sacrifice. She would see what he had given her and would fall in love at once. Their adoration, one for another, would shine like a street lamp, like a perfect neon sign.

So he rummaged through his own left wing, felt the quills as sharp as drinking straws, and yanked out a great flight feather. Then he limped through the air to the spot just above her head, flying lopsided and all unbalanced. He landed behind her, and still she did not see.

The magpie found himself in tears, despairing beyond measure, moved to insanity; moved to sacrifice. She might love him after his death; she would clutch a rose to her school shirt and cry for her lost one, who ruined himself just for the worship of her. With his face a silent caw of pain, he scissored through his own poor bone and grabbed his marvellous piebald wing in his beak; in one wide, giddy sweep, he dived from his perch, soared over the angel's head and dropped the gift from on high as he fell towards the tarmac, flying his last, now crippled forever. Now the wing was something the child did see, shining and twirling like a sycamore seed, and she almost reached out for it, but then her phone peeped and she looked in her bag.

Well, the song of the magpie is a very secret thing; rarer, more magical than the death-singing of swans, and sweeter and prouder than that of car alarms; the poor lame magpie still had this, his most secret thing, to give this child, this idol. And so, filling his chest with air and his heart with the purest music, the magpie lifted his little bullet head and began to pour out his love. Just then, the lights changed and she trotted across the road, peering at her phone.

THE ORGAN PRESS

Hᴇʀᴇ ɪs sᴏᴍᴇᴛʜɪɴɢ even mice cannot find, jammed in the shelf with the spine facing inwards. One might reach it from the top of the stool if one stood on one's toes. It is a great fat thing, a medical textbook; anatomy for the beginner, for the morbid child to wonder at and shudder over.

Between the pages, the cardboard organs: the layers of yellow and red and blue; the secretive workings of guts; the heart like velour in red and blue with hideous rubber tubing. One might pick that book up and spread it wide; the centrefold is where the belly bops right up, with stomach and ribs and mysterious spleen, with distended womb and a foetus inside, upside down, fists against his face and his modesty protected by the twist of umbilicus.

Inside the organ book, leaves within leaves; the flowers are waiting, marigold and poppy, bled of their colour, pressed by ancient children for making cards and bookmarks and forever since abandoned. They crowd the memory and the spaces between; the blue-cheeked forget-me-not and honesty between the curling bones of the ear; rose petals one by one against the dry salivary gland.

The hyacinth that seeped into the workings of the eyeball has left a mark like river water, retina and squishy lens horrified and perfectly still stopped as if by sudden disaster, aching like the singing of children.

The anemone is dreadfully fragile and can barely be moved, its vividness an elderly blue. To grasp at it, to try and move it by the stem would surely destroy it, would flutter it to broken bits like prayers against the great abnormal sky.

Turn the pages; every disease has its companion: carnations and bindweed's flower for the flex and tendons of the knee; throttled freesia for pleurisy and collapsing lung.

And here at last, between the split halves of brain, the softest of them all: the tender violet where the tumour holds itself tight like a tiny bud.

SLOW-MOTION

W HEN HER HEEL snapped off, when her ankle sprained
with a wrench and she gasped loud with the pain of it, she
thought that she could hear foxes crying. When she lost her
shoe, she balanced quite perfectly in the air like a snowflake,
like a maths equation.

When she put a hole in her tights her ears were shouting
with the lights from the night club. She had no time to make
herself ready, to smooth out her skirt or check her black reflection in the water. Her hair swished slower than shampoo com-
mercials and she felt weightless, almost not there.

Then her handbag hit the ground and fell open with a catastrophic jangle of keys, with lipstick and mirror and credit
card and a tiny sewn elephant with a bell. There was no saving
it now.

She listened to the river and its evil silence as her poise col-
lapsed; she found herself falling like a sack, waiting for the first
shock of water. When she lost her contact lenses, when her
mascara melted in the sudden bite of cold and wet, there was
nobody to see it but the angels, sharing a spliff and sniggering
at her, at her hopeless thrashing.

AFTER VAN GOGH

T HE VILLAGE IS bruised and bleeding blue and dark, grabbing and heaving like the sea. The night time cannot breathe; it flinches and yelps as if its ribs are broken, trying and trying to fill itself with air that's meaner than acid.

The stars are pulled-out teeth, rotten yellow, and the buildings crack and ooze like hot glass; the whole huge world bucks its back. Look, here, there's a massive thing like a black fire, yanking at the air, reducing what it can to charcoal. The pigeons are gathering on the squirming rooftops, holding on for dear life and wondering what it might mean, this tormenting, this endless suffering night. Even the pigeons cannot comfort it, however they try. It makes no sense to them.

When God is bored he stirs his great fat fingers in the world.

BIRTHING

WHILE YET THE massive universe is water, daylight thrums the lovely redness of the mother's skin. When the head is soft with finest down and liquid, it is time to be born. Open your eyes little one, for the last time gaze at the thrumming and the utter red.

For you are perfect, a whispered poem for the sky to hear, chanted over forty long weeks, ready at last to hatch. You are the secret songs of moles and rabbits, of dark and hidden things.

Stretch out and curl again, you tiny leaf, for your spine is sapling-pith, soft bending, and the world, this vast and vulnerable world, is for you.

THE BLACK WOOD

T HE BLACK WOOD is full of pin-sharp spatting rain, full of the laughter of crows. The black wood is drenched and freezing. The bark of every twig and bough is shiny-wet like blood on concrete, pointed and twitching with the wind. Between the trees there is only the sky, in scrags and tatters where clouds are tearing, low as the canopy, without a scrap of colour despite the overhead striplights. It's against reason; against bare sense. There is a dead forest in Tesco's.

The black wood has filled my mouth; I can taste the leaves, the damp, the metal tang of my own teeth. The forest creaks as it breathes out and in again and it stares at me so hard. I don't dare look back, so I grip the front of my trolley and shove it before me where the roots are tangled fingers and grip against the metal wheels.

The black wood was butchered for fires six centuries ago. There is nothing more to it now than its own colossal ghost, the force of its mind and the coughing of the crows. It is nothing but its soul now, dripping and naked, perfectly brittle.

And it makes no odds at all that the forest is gone, none at all, because the shiny floors are pierced like plastic with the trees, and the bracken thickens up my throat. I am pushing my way through it all, sinking over rot and leaf mould like teeth through soap.

At one o'clock in the morning, the girl on the tills has eyes as dark as bruises; I cannot tell if she has seen me. She is shivering. I glance at her sneakily, long and hard as I dare, because I don't want her to stare back. I'm not a stalker or anything, it's just that she is so young and so exhausted. She makes me sad. I wish I could make it better. *Come here,* I'd say, *have a rest for a minute. There's a blanket just there,* I'd say; *the manager is not here. I'll keep watch for you.* And I would, true as my word. The second a customer came I would tell her, but in the time between I would let the shop girl sleep. I would guard her from the crows and closing-time drunks. I look for an instant too long and she senses me, rubs at her mouth with the palm of her hand, snaps a glance at the clock on her till. There is such a pain in her.

I am tired as well, but I am too afraid for sleeping. The black wood is an ancient malice, a curse drawn with charcoal before the world's foundations were built, before ever a child was wrapped in a blanket or a fire burned in a grate. The black wood is here even now, solid as a car crash, puncturing the aisles and the ceiling, jabbing little twigs through the fridges where they keep the meat, leaking the smell of blood from every cling-filmed packet.

During the day I cannot come here at all, for then the place is violent with people, with trolleys and baskets and jumping children who graze their faces through the bramble thorns and don't even feel the scratch.

In the day time there are people holding washing powder in their bare hands, not knowing the wounds inside them as they're spiked with broken branches. At night there are only the crows and me, god help me; only me and the ghost of the

74

black wood, that knows it is dead and uprooted but does not give a damn for facts.

I turn my wrist sideways, try to slip my hand between the trees to pluck out a cold plastic box. I manage with hardly even a stammer 'til I'm almost through, but then a moth with wings like blanket tries to land against my finger. I jerk away against my will, even though I know I should stay calm. I drag my hand through the trees, right quick, and the box goes spinning along the floor.

Then the night clatters with the crows, with the high alarm cries of things unseen. Suddenly I am mobbed and flailing and I cannot bear it, cannot bear this shop, this life, the black wood. But the CCTV is watching me and I know the security man will come this way soon, with his unbrushed teeth and his arms that smell of flesh. So I hug my stomach and hold the sobbing in, and I crouch among the mulch and the bones until my hand finds the packet, and I brush it with the blunt of my thumb and catch it in my fingers.

When I get the box from the floor I hardly care what's inside it; the main thing is just that I have food to carry to the till. But I do look all the same; it is ham, square, marble-pink and vile. I drop it in the trolley and try to breathe.

Then I creep along the aisles, peering between the slabs of cheese and the trees that pull at my hair and my coat, trying to unhear it, the birds and the wind and the rain and the humming of the banks of freezers. I pick my way past the tin cans and the DVDs with hardly a thought in me, except that I must escape from this place. *I will be okay,* I tell myself; I'm only concerned with getting away, with buying my wretched square of ham and spinning through the automatic door. But first I have to pay. And that's how I find her, how I tiptoe right up to her and am smacked by her pain.

The girl behind the till looks at me as though I had flung ice in her face; when she locks her eyes with me, both of us flinch. She stares at me between the dripping branches as though I were a spectre, some fear of her own in an army-surplus overcoat, and when I try to speak to her, she cannot make my words out over the noise of the crows.

GONE

Once she turns the lights on, you can see right through the net curtains. When it gets dark, I look in the windows, at the magic lantern images behind that glass. Even when it's cold and raining, if I stare ever so hard without blinking, I can imagine myself warm, as if I was curled up on my mother's lap like a cat; or her knitting; or her child.

I used to live indoors. I had my own room, and my mother called me Anna. We lived that way for the best part of forever, my mother and me. I had scrambled eggs for my dinner, and I slept at night beneath a musty eiderdown that was spiky with the feathertips that stuck through its skin. I had been the sort of child that sat at her mother's feet every morning whilst she tugged at her daughter's hair with a brush and tied it into ribbons.

I began to wake up at night, afraid. At first I would wander to my mother's bedroom in tears, but I could never quite tell her what was wrong, and soon it began to annoy her. So, after a week or a fortnight, I would comfort myself in the dark, stroking my cheek and rocking.

It seemed to me that my bedding was killing me. I'd wake very slowly, pinned against my mattress, and I'd feel its press against my chest, the flat weight of it over my lungs. Every night for a month, my quilt grew more heavy; or else I grew more light. In the end, I found that I'd rather be cold.

My mother began to lose my focus, somehow; she sometimes stood and stared at me for a whole minute before she could think of my name. The first time, when she asked me what it was, I burst out laughing, and I told her it was Maggie Thatcher. When my mother shook her head, I giggled like a monkey, and called myself Lady Di. My mother did not smile, but walked away slowly as though she had come into a room to get something, but couldn't remember what it was.

She wasn't joking. I became frightened, and resentful; if she asked my name, I would shout at her and fight back tears, for I felt that she was cruel to pretend to forget me. In later weeks, however, I would step up like a salesman, right into her face, when she entered the room. *Hello,* I would say, *I am Anna and you are my mother,* and I would shove out my hand for her to shake. *Anna,* I'd repeat, *Who is your daughter;* and she'd take my hand lightly, barely, and let it go again before she turned away, moving her lips.

My mother began to neglect me; at suppertime, she'd lay one place instead of two, and sit by herself in the bright kitchen. She would stare at my empty dining chair with a face as sad as nothing at all. I would carrion-pick at her plate, stealing scraps; my mother would turn away and flail her hands at me as though I were a wasp.

If I left my nightlight on at bedtime, she would come into my room to switch it off. One day my mother walked right through me as I stood in her path; she knocked me flying, and tripped right over. She got to her feet, muttering, and she threw open the window for the January night to come in. The next day she stripped my bed and put my colouring books out for the bin men.

I took to sitting between her and the television, not that it made a difference; my mother would turn the volume up high, clucking sympathy with someone on *Coronation Street* and tutting at the news. Perhaps my body let light through these days. Over weeks, I learned the qualities of air; became the child-shaped draught that made my mother turn the radiators on full and wear her slippers with socks. I daren't look in the mirror in case there wasn't anything to see.

My mother thought the house was haunted when I shook her by the shoulders and threw things at her. I screamed in her ears and she'd cock her head as though she could almost hear. I wasn't as strong as I used to be; I picked and fluttered at the objects in the room, but I could hardly move them. Somehow, after an age of trying, I heaved the TV forward, flat on its face; the screen burst with a bang, and my mother fled the room. The effort half-killed me.

My mother went out all the next morning; she brought home a new telly and a dog. It was a Doberman, and it could see me all right; I fled the house with a long, bloodless gash where my wrist should have been. It's her guardian now; she calls it Gabriel, and feeds it scrambled eggs from her plate. She safe now; my mother is safe from me.

That's how I came to live out here; that's how I got so hungry. Eventually, though, some time soon, she'll turn on the lights, and I can spread myself flat against the windows, until you'd never know about the darkness at my back, because all I can see is the glorious colour of the armchair and the TV. Perhaps she will forget to switch it off at bedtime.

HELLFIRE

Back in the olden days when there were still flowers and butterflies and people, Satan's daughter lived with her daddy in the earth's rotten heart. Their home was a palace beyond compare: the veins pulsed in the marble walls; the floor was made of blunt red iron; the chandeliers were quartz and arsenic; and the stairs were carpeted with aluminium.

Every morning, the princess would look out from the diamond sheets that served the house for windows, and she would sigh. The landscape, for all its splendour, no longer made her happy. The Devil's daughter was older than stars, and lonely; her daddy was busy, and there was nobody to play with. His majesty had done his best; he had fashioned toys by the million, every one intricate and perfect, every one made from clockwork.

The princess spent her days beneath the bowl of the sky, breathing the sulphur breezes and trailing her hand in the fountain. There were fishes that swam in the mercury; they were quite tame, and would come sometimes to nibble at her fingers and jack-knife their tails.

One endless afternoon, as she lounged about morosely, a glitter of hummingbirds flashed over and began to feed from the nearby flowers. They were exquisite; still, their whirring annoyed her, and she shooed them away.

Quite by chance, the princess caught one in her hand; she felt the mechanism strain against the pressure of her thumb. Pinching her fingers either side of the creature, she opened her palm and held it close to her face. The poor thing began to flap, with one enamelled wing hanging off its torso. The Devil's daughter twisted the platinum hinge until it came off altogether.

The birdie opened its golden beak, and trilled out a burst of song, as it did every twenty-three minutes. On cue, the whole flock replied in unison; between them, they dashed off an eighty part harmony based on the tune of 'Oranges and Lemons'. Satan's daughter dropped the crippled humming-bird. It flew in little twirls until it strayed too close to the fish pool; a fat mechanical carp plopped up from the surface and polished it off.

She sat there for a long time, turning the tiny purple wing over in her hands, and thinking. She was not by nature a cruel child, but where was the place for love in a world where nothing had feelings? She could destroy the whole garden if she wanted, but there would be no blood and pain, just a heap of cogs and wheels and winding springs. She could go and ride her silver horse, and put her face against his great strong neck, but the horse wasn't a horse and cared not a bit for his mistress.

The Devil's daughter wandered back to the house, and on a whim, she stopped at the door of her father's office. It was ajar; she pushed gently until she could pop her head inside. Daddy was out on his errands. She crept up to his desk, and felt suddenly reckless. Reaching up on tiptoe, she took the handles of her father's periscope, and it descended with her pulling until she could sit down on the huge black chair.

What she saw made her weep. The world of men was alive and screaming with pain, and pity, and joy, and fear; and love, so much love that the people could barely stand it, and they died after only sixty or eighty years. She was fascinated; her yearning finally had shape. The daughter of Satan would go up to meet the people and share in their love. They would embrace her and adore her, and she too would die of love after only sixty or eighty years. She fled on weightless feet to the elevator.

It was locked; but the princess had seen her father leave for work every morning since the dawn of things, and she knew the number for the keypad. Inside, every surface was a mirror, and the Devil's daughter had half an hour to admire herself before the lift would arrive at the surface. Her eyes, of course, were sapphires, and her hair lay in thick auburn waves as far as her waist. Her wrists were long and narrow; she wore a fine uranium chain about her pretty throat. She smiled and sang to herself as she ascended.

And then she arrived. Satan's child was overwhelmed as she stepped out into the cold. She flung her arms about the waist of the first person she met; his cry was brief as he turned into cinders. The Devil's daughter was horrified, and she ran after the fleeing sons of men, pleading for love and shedding footprints of fire that set the street, and the city, and finally the whole earth alight. Her tears evaporated as she walked among the infernos, calling for anything that had a soul to come and be her friend.

TEST CARD F

S HE IS IMMORTAL, the girl on the test card, like some petty saint, patron of the fear of children. She smells of mummification and under-stairs tombs, all corners like Lego trod under the foot. She is decaying from the inside, taxidermy that she is, sawdust leaking from the rip at her armpit where skin and summer frock make a seam; she clamps her arm in hard to staunch it. '

Her companion is a clown, sewn shut at mouth and eyelids like a murdered shrunken head. The two of them are playing noughts and crosses, and it seems at a glance that one or other might be about to win, but this game has been going on for years, all these pitiless years.

The test card is the punishment for getting out of bed on Saturdays, when you creep downstairs like a very small spider, without the protection of your sister, when you do not understand how to read clocks but know it might be time for cartoons.

So you risk it, little heart jumping in your pyjamas and your socks; you crawl in front of the television; you crouch and brace yourself and turn it on.

She is waiting for you. She has always been lying in wait for you, with her Alice band and the smile of a dolly, and she injects your poor ears and your soul with the shrill and electronic note that accompanies her always, her and her giggling clown. Shuddering, twitching with fear, ears full to brimming, you skitter backwards on your heels and backside, and you get past the sofa and then you turn and run, chased all the way up the stairs, by the Test Card, by the long electric whistle that jabs your head like a spike.

SUFFOCATE

I AM SINKING. I have known this for three days; the grass in the park has become treacherous recently, after all that rain. The first time I walked on it, I put it down to the mud that sucked against my shoes. Complacent, sure of the solidity of things, I marched over the sodden lawn with scarcely a thought.

On my way home, though, it was dark and I was in a rush to get through before they locked the gates. I am afraid of the dusk and its duplicitous light. Already I regretted this shortcut; unformed danger reared up in the grey and vanished. A dog barked frantically and was answered by a whistle and a shout. I began to trot.

When I left the path I was sickened by the lawn, grown rotten with water, spongy. Its texture stayed with me all night, fattened my dreams. When I awoke, long before dawn, I was half drowned by my bedclothes and cold with sweat. I made coffee and resolved to pull myself together.

Friday was hot; I took the day off from work and sat for hours on a bench, watching the grass dry. Someone I knew came by and asked me if I was alright. I was. In the afternoon the students came out to shade their eyes and talk, and peer at their textbooks. When three separate groups were sitting on the turf, comfortable and chatting, I thought I would risk it. If they were safe, I reasoned, then so must I be. We were made of the same stuff, surely.

Warily, I trod out a few steps and stood, looking down. I had taken the precaution of wearing flat shoes. With vegetable slowness, the grass took hold and began to pull at my feet; with a gasp, I dived for the path. The students looked over, resumed their conversations. When I spread my palm flat and pushed at it, the grass was perfectly dry. When I got home I rang the council to report the problem, but I think they put the phone down on me.

The next day was Saturday, and by then things had got much worse. When I sat down on my settee it oozed like a quagmire, and before I had a chance to react, my lap had vanished into it. I flailed with my hands, clawing through the corduroy until I had a purchase on the wooden frame inside. My head sank into the cushion at the back and I tried to fill my lungs with hard-packed kapok before I managed to drag my face back through it into air. I sprawled onto the floor, shocked and coughing, my eyes and my throat thick with fluff.

After a long time, I got to my knees and stared at the sofa. The remote for the television had been knocked onto the floor, and I picked it up and dropped it onto a cushion. It fell lightly, bounced a little, lay still. I picked it up, dropped it again, and finally pounded the thing as hard as I could against the sofa's sprung belly. Nothing, except that the TV turned onto Ceefax and its stupid music. I pushed my fingers through my hair, and laughed out loud in panic.

It dawned on me then that the carpet was not stable. My shins had sunk by the tiniest margin; a millimetre, less. I scrambled upright, felt the deep pile drawing down like sand underfoot when the sea comes in. The lino in the kitchen was hard; I felt safer in there.

In the end, I spent the night on the table. At two o'clock in the morning I woke when my body fell through: I whacked my head against the floor. I think I broke a rib or two as well; it hardly matters. I fell through again an hour later, then it took forty minutes, finally only ten. There is a beauty to it, in a way; at the point of slipping though, if I am quick, I can see the table's grain, the secret soul of it bared for me during the instant when I cannot breathe. But now that I am tired of falling, I am sitting on the floor, perfectly calm, a slow swimmer through the things that are real, waiting to drown.

SOME LAST REQUESTS

Now that I have given up the ghost, now you are delighted to find my lovely piebald corpse, you must stretch me out, one wing and then the other, perfect like dawn light on slug trails. Pose me thus, for I always rather fancied crucifixion, not some common death on this grass verge. You must wash the blood off me, or else daub me all over with ink as red as sin, as the holy misdoings of a priest. I should like you to show me in the best light: magnificent I am, a nightmare to newly hatched creatures and small things.

Clip off one of my toes with secateurs, one that will not be noticed, and plant it in a little cup of earth, in case another magpie might spring from it, or a knobbly tree made of feet, the magpie growing in its compost upside-down. My remaining toenails may be painted, if you please; there is a window display on the Walk with all sorts of colours. I shall require the polish known as Raspberry Crush.

Oh yes, my feet are my crowning glory; twist them gently with copper wire, and twiddle me to a little bit of bark or the jawbone of a vixen. Make for me a lovely diorama: the prince of birds at bay. Do be sure to embalm me correctly, freeze my blood vessels with your nice warm fluids, the white towels and the metal things for grasping and incising.

Ah, but why stop there? Goodness me, why stop there?

Let's go all avant-garde! Electroplate my wonderful beak with a thick gilt coat and replace my shrewd little eyeballs with mother of pearl. Slice me crossways and protect my tender stuffings with gut-stitch. When I am a sculpture of curls with two fabulous wings, I shall require two axolotl gills, which are perfect as foliage; I demand metallic fins like those of the seahorse, all in silver plate and broken jewellery.

I shall wear bits and pieces of other creatures, their carapaces and their colours; I shall wear their fractured beauty across my own distended belly, my wonderful feathered tail like a fan for a paramour.

PHOENIX

THIS IS HOW the phoenix became. It began with sparks, which fizzed and flashed in a plug socket until the casing turned to glue. The television sagged, spineless with fear when the plastic oozed, for then a little blue flame slid out from the gap, scuddered over the carpet and ran itself to nothing like a crayon.

For five whole minutes there was not much doing; the electrics spat out an ancient curse, and a sleazy roll of smoke unravelled slowly, turned the air greasy. A mouse whispered to her children in the dark and wondered.

On top of the gas fire was a china pony, a dirty teacup and a red onyx egg; this last a gift from Italy. Inside, a heartbeat ticked, slow and wily as a tar pit. Some embryos will wait for centuries to hatch. The smoke slid against it, and it stirred. A maze of veins began to form in time-lapse and a glob of flesh grew head and feet. The mice listened to its pulse and prayed to the god of mice; nobody answered.

Beside the rocking chair, the socket spluttered so hot that it began to burn. The first licks of fire jumped upward, scarring the wallpaper until one plucked at the curtain and the hem caught with a cough, turning the fire from blue to yellow. In half a minute more, a lump of flame fell from the velveteen and set the sofa going with a stink of melting foam.

The stone egg heaved, forth and back, until it shunted the china pony to the floor; then, its path cleared, it threw itself off. It hit the hearth tiles with the sound of a breaking skull, and rolled along the carpet, feeling through its shell for where it was hottest. The mice squeezed flat and fled through the gap under the living room door.

When the window broke, the fire took a very deep breath; there was silence for a beat and then the night rushed in and the flames began to bawl. The stone egg hatched and a chick struggled free from its shell. Its feathers dried quickly, and presently it sat upright and raised its head. Its eyes were green and cold as cold.

The firebird shook its filthy down and chirped for flesh. The blaze fed it a picture book and a molten dolly. The telephone became a gorgeous waxy pulp before it charred. The house fire snapped its jaws and ran yelling up the stairs; sirens began to wail from the high street. The firebird wiped its beak against the floor and basked, growing bigger all the time. In half an hour there was nothing in the universe but fire, and sharp flight feathers burst out from its wing.

You could see the house's sinews once the ceiling caved in, bitten and glowing and thin as sticks. The firebird preened its tail, and admired itself in the blue-bright strobing lights. It was beautiful, serene almost, silent in the terrible chanting of fire.

When there was nothing left to scrape but joist and lintel, the blaze chewed out its own belly. When the fire crew got close there was hardly a thing to save. It was then that the phoenix finished hopping up the ruined staircase and spread its wonderful feathers. Through a breach in the roof it fledged, a smiling mirage.

HERE, EVERYTHING IS
STILL FLOATING

W ITHIN THE FOUR-SQUARE edges of our world we hang, like flies in a web: now trembling, now resigned; then shuddering again. One might consider us without purpose, but do not misunderstand; our inertia had made us immortal. We save ourselves like vials of lovely poison, all claret colours and rarity, gorgeous as ruby when held against the light.

And so we look, from horizon to empty-brained horizon for instructions, for some neat key to make us decipher this life. Anything would do, like the picture on the jigsaw lid that unjumbles the jumble of the pieces. *We are cats curled up in a basket of knitting,* we might say, or there again, *Look, we are the waves of the sea and a ship is sinking among us to its new drowned bed.* We would know, for certain; we would know and would adjust ourselves accordingly.

So we sit out eternity with our cooking stoves and our ill-lit parlours, rocking to and fro in the skinless light, tapping with our fingers the piano-key exercises that we learnt long ago. We read the newspaper every day; by now the writing is smudged to abstraction, grey ghostish letters on grey paper. It is no painful task to read it, not anymore, for the news is not legible, however catastrophic. We do not care to sully our heads with the idiot monsters of childhood. Indeed, our smiles and our light-bulbs are so interchangeable that there is no darkness left in the world, just shadows; only shadows. We gaze at one another, and we nod.

We float like fishes in the sky, you and I, like some ancient party balloon, surely one bound for somewhere, our brains fermenting beneath our hats. We are useful for nothing, figurines on a mantelpiece, lifeless and deathless both. Our entrails are slowing, ready for repainting, for the anatomist to count our bones, to lay them apart with his tender knife. Our eyes, already lidless, are drying nicely.

Listen to the clock's elderly tick-tick; hear your moments sheared off one by one. They clutter the narrow landing; they thicken the air and make the carpet musty, merciful like a face swathed in cloth. Eke out your death with us my dear, among the tea things and the plates.

ANTI-CLIMAX (OR THE END OF A GAME)

T HE GAME ENDS thusly, with the Zero card; the Joker, the Fool, split from his pack but laughing, face up in the gutter. Leave him there without a pang of guilt as he swills in spirals, sinking very slowly.

The game ends thusly: the narrow grinning of the Joker, past redeeming, the shine lifting from his smile. He turns the world into a joke, a fragile transfer as the cardboard melts, witness to the shining of puddles, reflector of street lamps and their grudging lights.

The game ends thusly: without winner or shaken hands, just the grin of the Fool and the soggy pastry oblong where he used to cling, idiot's cap and silent bells. At ten to eleven he comes right away; if it were not for the soggy leaves and filth in the gutter he might have gone down the storm-drain. But the fates take pity on the poor old Fool for a little while longer, for there's nothing at all in his head, despite the curl of his lip and his very natty costume.

The game ends thusly: when the temper is lost and the cards are thrown into the sky, stratosphere and heavens and the earth, God's enormous card table. They land in their various places, with only the players to divide the spoils, smiling viciously one to another, clutching handfuls of plastic chips, not one of them worth a thing.

THE OPPOSITE OF FALLING

AND AT LAST it comes to this, the heavy tread past drain covers, where the gulls cannot be comforted and the gutters are full to their gullets. The bus spills people out at the allotted stop, dawdles a while, then sways away from the kerb. There are lights showing in the windows; it is late and everyone is tired.

The night is winding the city like tangled hair. The sky will be whitish for half an hour more. The moon is thin as a retina. The pavements are shining. There is glory of a sort.

He hugs his burden like a creature cursed, forced by gods to be torn open every day, or made to roll some impossible rock to the shoulders of a mountain. He is guarded, the man with suitcases, haggard in his resignation; his eyes are hooded like a crow's or some such scapegoat. He has made his choice. His coat is sodden from the rain, and it weighs on him like a secret. His breathing stands in the air as he passes.

Oh but the luggage is heavy. The footfalls of the suitcase man are slowing, nearly scuffing the ground. The pigeons regard him as he toils past them; they make a little path for him as he goes and they coo for him and his sadness.

The wind is fiddling with the brim of the suitcase man's hat, which is brown and made of felt. Perspiration wets his neck. He is trembling with exhaustion now as he turns right, passes the Travelodge; despite his gritted teeth, the suitcase man has to stop for a beat. He shifts his fingers where they grip the handles, away from where the blisters are, and it helps a little, but he daren't let go.

The suitcase man closes his eyes and then he opens them, watching himself enter the car park's great square maw. He daren't use the lift for he can't let go of his burden, not even long enough to press the sticky buttons. So he begins to shuffle along the ramps, against the roar of invisible traffic, ghosts of motion. Some signs are yellow and some are green and red; huge arrows indicate the direction of flow. He is not travelling in the correct direction. The face of his wristwatch glints in the sodium lights. Level 1; Level 2; level 3; Level 4; grey as cement.

At the roof the air is lashing at the coat of the suitcase man, billowing against him as if he were a mote of nothing, as if heaven itself has a mind to pluck him from the skin of reality. And maybe it has. The suitcase man holds his gaze against the endless sky, screws his eyes at it, and drops his cases, one-two.

They bang against the floor and one clatters open, shedding its contents. It has been filled to its oblong skin with metal things: knives and forks, bagsful of nuts and bolts, weights from a gymnasium, the head of a sledgehammer. It is, was, ballast, it tethered him to the ground like the opposites of wings. Now he is ready to die, to lift forever from the earth, to find the place where even the angels would suffocate, to the cold white brilliance of death. Now that it hardly matters he rubs his sore hands against each other, adjusts his hat and his spectacles and feels the twilight sky dragging on him until he is nothing but flight itself; nothing but a mark against the cloud.

PIGLET

*J*ACKY'S IN THE *garden. Every morning the early dew wets his eyes, and the birds sing to him with their histrionic voices. His rockers are broken. He does not mind.*

I'd been in the house for ages before I got around to tackling the garden. First, there was the wrench of moving; when I finally beached up in my own front room, I lay on the floor for a whole day, breathing. There was no noise to follow me now, only the sound of my own lungs. It freaked me out after a while, so I put the radio on and sang out loud to Razorlight whilst I painted the kitchen yellow.

I got blood on my sampler when I pierced my fingertip; Nurse said that I should have put the blood into my mouth, rather than bleed upon my work. I did not care to swallow my blood however, and so a thick brown stain spread over the linen where I stitched my name. Every night in the nursery Jacky watched me sleeping with his wide and painted stare.

I only really found it by chance, when I decided to dig out that hideous lilac that was taking up half the garden. I'd bought a couple of rose bushes, sad little twigs in black plastic pots; they looked completely dead to me. I wasn't really sure of what I was doing; I wondered even if the woman at the garden centre had ripped me off. I had a vague idea you had to plant new things in early spring; at any rate, hacking back the lilac had seemed an impossible task in the heat of the summer. Instead I snuck up on it in January, and sawed through its tortured stalks with a bread knife.

Jacky was Emily's; all my things had been. I was born after the tragedy; in a fashion I suppose I was born through it. To be conceived because of death is a terrible thing. The second room in the nursery was Emily's; frozen in the minute she left it, holding its breath until she scampered in to fetch her hoop. When I was old enough to be Emily, the new Emily, Mama came with Nurse to show me the room that was now mine. Jacky stood in the corner, still as a coffin with his bright teeth smiling. I remained in the doorway, and had not a word to say. Nurse grasped my shoulders in her hands and pushed me into the new Emily's place; I took a tripping sort of step forward, then caught my balance and turned to face my mother. Mama's face was shining and little wild. I looked from her to Jacky, at their glazed, beaming faces.

That lilac was a sod to dig out. Since I'd got the place I'd made myself promises about making a start on the garden. The estate agent had said it was a blank canvas, and we'd looked at it with him and been thrilled. It was our investment, this place, 'til it all went belly up and I got lumbered with the mortgage. Blank my foot. It was a thicket of elder and bramble thorns and that monstrous lilac. But the last thing I wanted was some sweaty bloke in my space, looking me up and down and scratching his belly.

I did not make a good Emily. I was too tall for my age and thick of frame. The housekeeper used to call me Piglet; I

*heard her often when passing the kitchen door. I am not given
to scampering, and my hair is brown. I would not play with
Emily's things. At night there was Jacky, watching me in the
darkness.*

After a whole day of lopping off branches, I decided that a
bonfire was called for. I was quite excited; I'd never made a fire
before, and the notion made me feel naughty, somehow, like a
child playing grown-ups. My house; my fire. My stupid, too-
big, chilly house. I began to haul the brushwood together to
form a stack, with his old leather jacket and some books from
before in its guts.

*I resolved to become the housekeeper's Piglet, in the hope
that I should not fit Emily's clothes, nor the empty hole in the
world that she had left. I tiptoed into the larder late at night,
and cut myself slices of pie and slivers off the ham, and I would
sip at the jug of cream and try to will myself into a new shape.*

*After a while of forcing my body like some poor beast
awaiting slaughter, I found that I had formed a habit for it.
Nurse would stand me before the mirror and scold my glut-
tony. If I had ever seen her, Nurse would say, her light-footed
beauty, then I should be ashamed. Emily had not been a child,
but an angel, Heaven's brief gift. The housekeeper would
smirk as she let out my dresses at the seams.*

There was a little parcel tied to a stalk by a slimy bit of
ribbon. I was thinking *Blair Witch* here, but still my curiosity
overtook me, and I squatted in the mud to open it. At first I
thought it was a tiny collection of twigs, but as I tipped it into
my hand, I saw a skull and a little pointed beak. I threw it
away from me with a horrible shudder.

One day we had guests, and when mama made me stand

before the piano, I chose to bray out the genteel song that Nurse had forced me to learn. Drink to me Only, *I cried like a donkey, and the guests became quite silent and the maid looked at the floor and smiled.*

All that day and the next, I uncovered little bundles like the first. They gave me the jitters, and at night I found myself nervous, alone in my tall house. I rang Jo but she had gone to Brighton for the weekend; I nearly phoned my mother but thought better of it. Instead, I kept the bonfire going and threw the packets in as soon as I found them.

Emily had not been a tidy creature, Every evening after prayers I set myself to the task of clearing Emily away from our room. At first I disposed of only the smallest items; I fed her pressed flowers to the oil lamp, and her velvet bookmarks, one by one. I took the scissors from the kitchen and hid them beneath Jacky's rocker; the housekeeper raged and searched for them for a whole week. Eventually the maid was dismissed for their theft. I cut the edges from Emily's Lord's Prayer, inch by inch, and every night I burned them in my little light.

There was a birdcage that hung by Emily's window. Its prisoner was called Gideon. He was terribly old, and Nurse said he had never sung since the passing of Emily. One day, an inspiration struck me, and I caught him in my hand and felt the flutter of him against my fingers. I took a lace handkerchief from Emily's lavender drawer, and placed Gideon in the centre. I made a little bundle, like a pomander, with the bird in its middle instead of cloves. Then I crept into the garden and tied him in the lilac. I muddied my nightgown and earned a chiding from Nurse.

There were times, I will own, when fear crept into my heart by night. If I was not to be Emily, I pondered, then might I be nobody at all? In my dreams I sat upon Jacky, sprawled over his back with my cheek against his mane like some dead child. I could neither get up, nor close my dull, blank eyes.

Those bloody packets started to give me nightmares.

It took me days before I could even see the soil. I looked at it, wet and black. Someone else might have been able to gaze at it and say, *My, what lovely rich loam.* Not me; I had no bloody clue. It might have been poisonous as far as I could tell. Still, it clearly needed digging, so I tied up my hair, shoved in a fork with the sole of my shoe, and started to lever up tangled roots in knots.

When the fork hit something in the ground I felt sick; my first thought was that it might be a corpse; some ancient skull or casket.

Eventually Nurse could see that there was something afoot. In a sudden rush of observation, she saw that there were many things of Emily's that were no longer in the room. The canary! The dolls! The books! She shook me and demanded to know where they were. I said that Emily had taken them back. She called me a wicked, wicked child. Nurse slapped my face and said that my father should be summoned to the house to hear of this.

Nurse told me of the suffering of my dear mother, and said that for all she cared, I should be sent to bedlam for my evil heart, for I was surely mad. I looked at my Nurse, and then all the way through her. I went slowly to my bed and lay there, very still beneath my eiderdown. Nurse stared after me in silence, then strode away.

When I yanked the fork out, there was a streak of white

paint on it. I sank to my knees and began to scrape at the soil with my fingers.

As I was no longer truly real, I found myself possessed of a passion of sorts, though calm enough of mind. I gazed about the room and felt Jacky's stare upon me, and knew that he must be the last and greatest thing that I should exorcise. I threw the window wide, and with a great deal of effort, managed to put him through it. Then, it being already dark, I crept outside to the place where he had fallen.

After half an hour it was uncovered: a rocking horse, buried on its side in the dirt by the back wall. The rockers were broken, and it was painted a flaking dapple grey. Its mane and tail had decomposed. It beamed at me from the ground, frozen in mid-prance, with carved wooden flowers on its bridle. I stood up and began to back away from it.

When I had done with Jacky, one might not have known that he ever was. I tucked him into the earth beneath the lilac bush, concealed and safe, and with just his face exposed so that he should be able to breathe. I covered up his smile with leaves and returned to my bed to wait.

I went to sleep that night with the lights on. When I pulled the duvet over my head it was as though that horse was in the room with me, creaking forwards and back again on its broken rockers and smiling.

THREE CHILDREN ARE MENACED
BY A NIGHTINGALE (AFTER ERNST)

How do nightingales menace children? Nightingales fly alone, like murderous flapping moths; they are attracted to children as blow flies are to offal. Their hearing is splinter-sharp; they can hear a baby breathing from a street away.

A figure is leaping, up on the roof of the little red house, over the hut where the foxes and the chickens live side by side in dollies' cots and tell each other stories from the old country. The hens are kindly as grandmothers, and they cluck their disapproval of the man upon their roof, for he has, tucked against his chest, close as a stolen thing, a baby. Her eyes are empty and black as a treacle tin, her wailing enough to break one's heart.

Perhaps he has gathered her up to carry her to safety, or else to keep her for his own, like a dropped fiver. If he runs hard enough he might shove his way behind the picture frame which holds the scene like a window, to the huge invisible world behind it and the woods, the endless, aching woods.

How do nightingales menace children? With the beauty of their singing, dripping like poison, sharp as vodka. They dive for the eyes as crows will, with sharp and silver tongues, with their legs like coat-hanger wire. They get in close, as if to kiss, and they steal the singingness, the musical souls of the very young. Without singing, a child is not alive at all, just a husk in ringlets; a husk in blue pyjamas.

Sometimes a nightingale might make it past the flapping curtains, and all there is for poor Mama to discover is a sad little thing, curled like an onion skin, silent before she ever sang, before she knew life or music or anything.

With her beak full, the nightingale sweeps to her own infants, all of them trembling with silence, and stuffs the singingness into each, every one brittle and lovely as frost; they strop their beaks against one another till they're sharp as the pegs on a musical box.

But look! One child has already fallen, overcome by the loveliness which serves as chloroform, pierced in the throat and lapped dry. He is a sea shell; a broken toy or dead cocoon. His soul is perfectly mute.

But here, where the evening is settling into layers like Guinness, blue till yellow in the sky, Brillo-pad green for the turf, the last child stands aghast with something in her hand, whilst the nightingale hovers above her. The chickens from the little red house are clucking thorough the windows: *come child; here child,* calling her to where it's surely safe, amongst the nests and feathers and warm corners.

The foxes are not so sure, for the parents of children are known to murder foxes and rob chickens, to steal the beautiful eggs of the morning time, but still they join in with the calling: *Come here, child; come here, sweetheart, we will protect you, only come!* But she cannot hear, the third child, for the calling of the nightingale is sweeter and louder than the shouting of chickens.

AT THE SHOW TRIAL

T HE BLUE DEER stretches out his voice to bark at the air between the branches, wet as blackness, thinner than thinking. Hummingbirds flit like wild ideas, counter-notes to the sky's gigantic pulse.

The afternoon holds the forest like an X-ray, shows up the hollow chest of the ash tree and the sickness of elm, the filaments and veins. And so it is that the canvas of the earth is pinned, edge and line and tragedy: the laughter of rooks and the sobbing grey compassion of pigeons. Here is the very first shock of seeing, when the eyes unclose at birth or the eggshell is broken; when the embryo gawps at the glory of the world and finds itself born. Oh but it hurts, this sudden clarity with the cellophane of oneself squashed so, with the judder of the heart so loud in the ears. Here is the eternal expose, when the sins of the universe are held up to daylight to be counted.

The mouse holds the least guilt. She asks little from God beyond a scrap here and there and a corner safe from cats. She sees the whisker-tremble of her own nerves, a life made out of cheese rinds and fear. She ponders her tiny self, dusty and delicate as lace.

Starlings come next; their greedy beaks are spiked with hunger as they jab at the poor world. They drag the earthworms from their innocent tunnels, snap them down like kitchen tongs, hardly caring for their sorrow. They stick and stab at the mud; they congregate in great guttural mobs; they line up on the telegraph wires like little vultures.

But we are hungry, they cry, *and besides we are beautiful, with wing-feathers bright as blades and secret colours. God made our nature*, they cry; *our nature is no-one's fault but his.* Their eye's glitter like coal and are perfectly black. Beneath the universe's glare they aren't too bad, and the murder of a worm is barely a murder at all.

Dog comes fawning into view, coward's tail between his legs, trying to conceal his teeth behind his grinning lips, choking down the thousand rabbits that he has ripped to bits. They gather at the door of his throat with the billion little creatures that he bites down on in his dreams, when his legs twitch against the carpet and he seems to be running.

The universe is watching and the dog is heaving his belly, gorged and grappling with lifetimes, with so many tiny killings, with garbage and dog meat from tins. They bulge in his belly, barred by his teeth, little broken ghosts, wild eyed and clutching their fragments about themselves. And dog discovers what he is, ravenous and desolate, an eater of souls.

WINTER AT HOME

W E DID NOT see the signs, not in those first days of winter. The cold crept in at the joints of the windows, seeped into the damp carpets. Molecules of ice swarmed the hallway.

My mother and I did what we could, stocking the larder with tins and powdered milk. At the caustic end of November the sun barely rose at all, loitering pale and ineffectual at the corners of the mornings and dwindling to a rumour of light by four.

The last time my mother left the house she came in as chilled as death himself. I rubbed at her stiff arms and she drank cocoa until she had warmed into her body like the spreading of ink through water. By the next morning we could not open the front door at all; it was rigid and braced in its frame. We gazed out of the window and watched a layer of frost craze the pane until all that we could see was the phantom of our faces reflected back at us. The house grew dark.

I was afraid; a worry began to snag on my nerves when I lit the fire in the evenings. If we used the gas greedily, I feared that the bottle would run out, and then where would be? I always took on the task myself; with solemn care I would turn on the gas, my lit match at the ready, and flinch sideways when the blue flame whoofed and licked its front. It was a poor thing, weak as water against the furnace of the cold.

We passed a month walking from room to room, lost under coats and sweaters, faceless to each other. My mother would pace endlessly, her head on one side and her bones creaking like corroded springs. After two more weeks, we ran out of matches; I hauled for a pointless hour against the back door, but it would not budge.

My mother and I grew torpid, slowing in the manner of insects, sluggish and gentle as paralysis. It was my mother who began to freeze first. The first signs were the crystals of ice that began to accumulate in the corners of her eyes. She would rub and rub at them with the heels of her hands.

Over hours a film of frost began to cover my mother's eyes, cracking and reforming every time she blinked. In three more days, my mother stopped blinking; sharp cataracts blurred her vision to a vague blueness. I wrapped her in coats, blankets, the curtains even but she rattled and chattered so much that they kept falling off. The china vase in the parlour broke in that week. It jumped with a start like a dropped teacup, the cold too much for its poor porcelain.

My breath began to take a form of its own, flagging from my mouth at first, but as the winter increased its gnawing, it would form into crystals that fell to the ground, or into my lap as I sat with my mother. Our conversations evolved into brittle flowers that strewed the carpet and crackled under our feet.

We sat in the evenings with baskets on our laps to catch the words, lest they should melt upon our clothes. Before another week had passed, the sounds themselves were quite encased in ice, and our speech was reduced to the glassy tinkle of crystals falling one against the other. Those that fell upon the floor tended to burst when trodden on, such that they would suddenly give up a sound when broken open. Our footsteps played out a sort of fractured speech, a 'this' or a 'how' or 'perhaps', a poetry of despair. Still, we continued to talk to one another, for what else had we to do to amuse ourselves? When the tap water stopped flowing I collected frozen talking for the electric kettle; the rest piled up in heaps.

Our abstract conversations eventually began to slow, and then to cease altogether as the hinge of my mother's jaw grew gradually less able to move. One day, close to what must have been Christmas, no snowflake noises came from her at all. My mother's mouth worked dryly like a rusted machine. She had become mute.

I cleared the ice around her nose and mouth that collected as she breathed. I tried and tried to pry open my mother's lips to feed her spoonfuls of tepid cocoa. It was not so very long until her jaw stuck like an iced-up lock.

The tin cans became metal rocks. I made myself endless cups of cocoa, without milk when the milk ran out, but as soon as the scalding liquid cooled enough for me to wrap my hands around the mug, it was frozen and hard as a stone. I lost a dozen teaspoons that way. I had to take care to let go of the cup in time, lest my palm should stick against its frosted outside.

My mother soon grew as hard as hard; only her eyes moving inside their icy covering showed any flicker of life. Bitten with guilt, I decided I must salvage the blankets for my own self, as she seemed to be so beyond repair.

I tried to lift the blankets and coats from my mother's body, but everything was frozen such that the blankets and my mother were all of one huge piece, and so very heavy that I confess I dropped them.

My mother shattered. I stood and stared in horror at the strata of flesh and bone, blanket and skin that striped the pieces in cross section like a marble cake. Numb to my soul, I emptied out a basketful of words; they fell to the floor like lightbulbs, releasing a quick and deafening shout as a hundred unsaid things were all spoken at once. I gathered all the bits of my mother from the metal-hard carpet and placed them in a corner of the room, arranging unlit and unlightable candles around the basket like some futile reliquary. One glassy splinter had cut my hand. The small red bubble that welled up became a jewel when I pried it off my finger. I laid it with care upon the mantelpiece, and took my mother's place in the armchair.

HOLIDAY

GOD'S CLEANING LADY was called Rosa; for a fiver an hour she came over on Mondays, Wednesdays and Fridays to do the kitchen and vacuum the house. Rosa was tired; her hair was damp after the sleety walk from the bus. She stopped at the top of the stairs, lugged the Dyson onto the landing in front of her, and waited whilst she caught her breath. The low table and the mirror needed dusting again, the stuffed lamb's head too; she'd have to come up here again and spray its glassy eyes with polish. This staircase was never used. There were no visitors to God's house any more; interviews were not granted.

There were always pickets outside God's house though: evangelicals; animal rights people; bereaved parents with huge silent eyes. One man came every day for fifty-six years, to prop himself up with a placard on a stick. It had proclaimed that *GOD IS LOVE;* the rainwater and sunlight bleached it so much that in time it faded to an agnostic grey. One day, he didn't show up.

The carpet had once been triumphant scarlet; it had worn down in patches as far as the hessian; too many years of dirty shoes had caked between the fibres until the floor was the colour of kidneys. The walls in God's house were stained and creeping with mould, and the doors let the draughts in.

Today was the last day, and Rosa had a cold; she pulled

a hankie out of her sleeve and blew her nose. She smiled at her reflection in the mirror, and buttoned up her cardie. After months of dreaming, she had finally made her decision. Twenty-two years, and never a thank-you: Rosa had had it up to here. Just once more, she thought, just this once, she would try to make this awful house look better. At that, a jar of nerves made her look away from herself. Rosa hauled on the Dyson's flex and unravelled a few feet of cable. She held onto the dado rail whilst she jammed the plug into the wall, and then Rosa blew her nose again, and stooped to press the ON button.

God had never noticed the people who stood at his front door because he never looked out of the windows; the old man had retired here to wait out his trillion-year dotage. He sat in his bedroom all day long, arguing with himself and smoking Superkings in his nightshirt. A girl came in the mornings to haul him from his bed. Rosa heard her sometimes, speaking up so he'd hear, asking him to sit forward, or swing his legs so she could help him into a chair. More often, Rosa would hear him shouting at her. Rosa's mouth was a tight pink line as she took the head part off the cleaner and began to suck dust from the shabby bannisters. An ancient spider clambered over the wing of a stuffed dove. Rosa looked at it for a while, then sighed and let it be.

By half past four, she'd made a start on the kitchen. The rain was plastering down the window, and it was getting dark. Rosa had pled with the housekeeper for ages for stainless-steel worktops, but she would have none of it. After a half-hour scrubbing at the pitted wooden table, Rosa emptied the dustbin and mopped the lino. Then she washed the alpine stink from her hands, picked up the roll of bin bags, and peeled one off.

Her fingers were almost steady. She pressed them together for a moment, tip against tip: Rosa's hands were short and square. She folded the bag to a flat black oblong, and stowed it in her apron pocket. As an afterthought, she pulled down the flaps of flypaper and collected up the rat traps, and threw them all away.

When she'd gone for the job, donkeys' years ago, it had been made clear that she was to keep to herself; she'd never had any dealings with Mr Lord directly. Today, though, she wanted to see him, just once, to take her secret leave of God and his crappy house. Rosa smoothed her skirt over her knees and crept like a little girl to stand outside the sickroom.

She stopped at the door; it was ajar. Rosa stood back and gazed upon the face of God. His great cropped head was prickly with hair the colour of fibreglass. His eyes were wild and blue, and blind; God had lost his sight centuries ago. He was propped with pillows into a tall wing-backed chair, muttering to himself in an empty room. His eyebrows rose and fell with every sentence; for no obvious reason, God began to laugh. Rosa held her breath and edged away from her Creator's presence. He didn't notice.

Just after five, Rosa wrote a note on the back of her time sheet and left it pinned to the scullery door. She unfolded her plastic bag, and felt her cheeks burning as she entered God's dingy cloakroom. When she left the house, Rosa clutched an awkward package inside her coat and scurried through her foggy breath for the bus shelter.

The bus that stopped at God's house was all but empty; a televangelist got on behind Rosa. He was shivering. She could smell him; he'd probably been sleeping rough in God's front garden for days. She regarded him sidelong; there was studio make-up collected in the folds of his neck and around his sincere, compassionate mouth. He cleared his throat.

Rosa turned away, feigning deafness, watched the industrial estates and run-down terraces slide past. She focussed on the sky, and discovered that she was perfectly calm. The evangelist got off at the next stop; a microphone was clipped to his tie, the black wire attached to nothing at all.

Rosa's tenement block wasn't far from the bus stop. She stood in the lift with her handbag and black-wrapped package; a tear had developed in the plastic, and a mushroomy scent was leaking from the hole. Rosa clamped her hand over it.

The lift smelled of high-rise housing and sick. Today, Rosa breathed deeply in that yellow cube of air, savoured its horribleness, and committed it to memory. She took note of the greasy buttons, and the layered fly-posters and marker-pen tags. One had been done in silver ink, and it was new. As the lift whined skyward, Rosa peered at it. It seemed to say *JAMAICA*. Rosa nodded thoughtfully; Jamaica was certainly a good idea, or Spain at the very least.

In her bedroom, Rosa shut the curtains; they billowed in against the balcony window. She could hear the dull bass-line of a distant stereo. Rosa picked up her plastic sunglasses from the dressing table, and from the bag she shook her new wings. They were great things, heavy as a coat, not exactly beautiful but patterned like a tabby cat.

The wardrobe had a long mirror on the inside of the door; when Rosa had fitted them across her shoulders like a brindled feathered waistcoat, she found that she could admire herself as she beat them gently in the air, her shoes an inch or two from the floor.

Very carefully, moving like a child on a new bike. Rosa flew upwards until she could reach the suitcase on top of the wardrobe, and lowered herself until she hovered above her bed, as she gathered up sun cream, a nightdress, a faded bikini, and three clean headscarves.

ACKNOWLEDGEMENTS

THANKS TO DORRIE Young, who saved my life, to my agent, Victoria Hobbs and to Kate Pullinger; love to Simon Blue, Das Fenster, George Szirtes and the wonderful Helen Ivory. Thanks to the Bridges writers, especially Hilary Mellon. Love to Naomi and Bharat, and massive thanks to everyone at Salt.

NEW FICTION FROM SALT